ISBN 978-1-928161-64-6

Jim Nash The Beginning is a work of fiction. Any resemblance to persons living or dead is purely coincidental. Places mentioned by name are entirely fictitious and purely products of the author's imagination, and are not meant to bear resemblance to actual places or locations.

Publisher: P X Duke

Web site: pxduke.com

E-mail: peterxduke@gmail.com

Cover image: Layers Pixabay

9 8 7 6 5 4 3 2 1

Printed in the United States of America

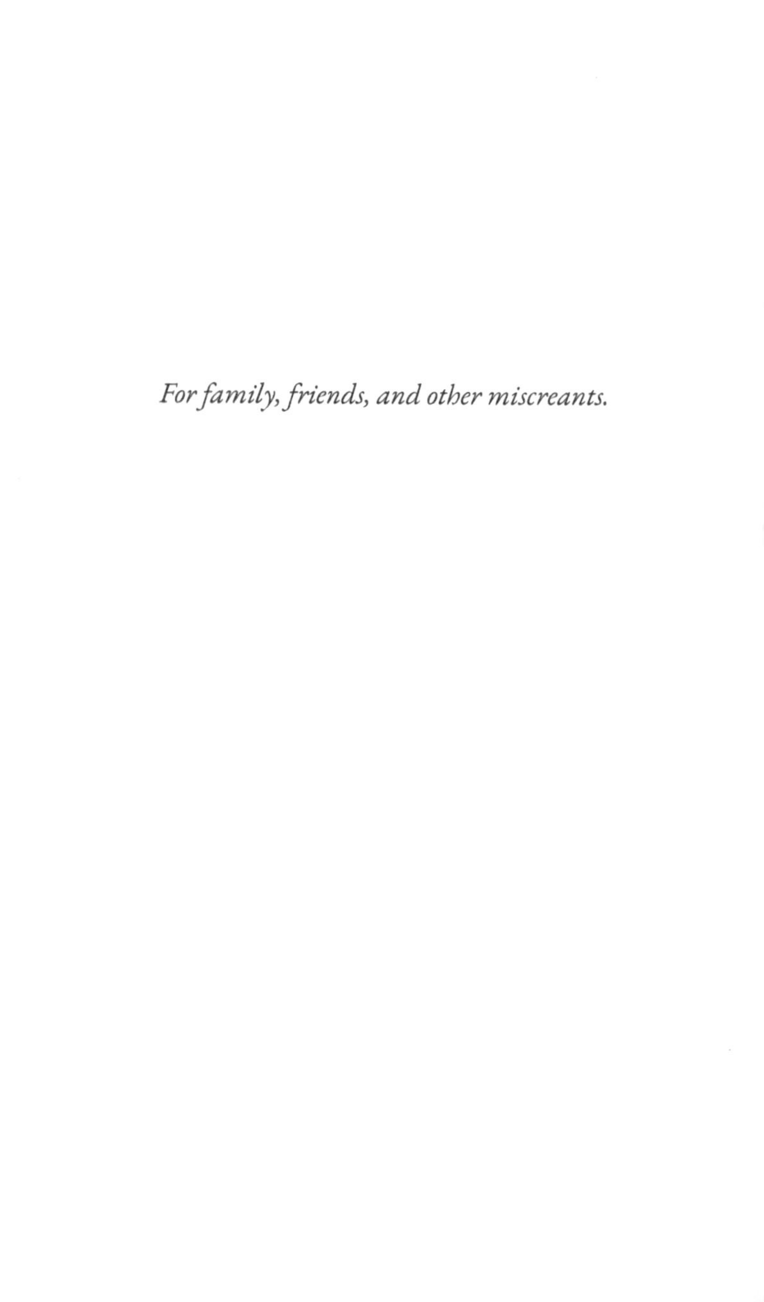

For family, friends, and other miscreants.

THE BEGINNING

JIM NASH

PX DUKE

JIM NASH

THE BEGINNING

Marina Mystery - 1

A dead body introduces Detective Jim Nash to Coroner Allie Sands. Despite warnings from just about every woman working in the same building, Allie throws caution to the winds while helping Jim solve a murder. As their relationship deepens, someone is intent on digging a grave for Jim deep enough that he will never climb out.

Twisted Sisters - 43

Police Detective Jim Nash has two murder victims. His own homicide division wants to charge him with murder. To say he's got serious commitment problems would be an understatement. He's on the lookout for twins, but he doesn't want to date them. He wants to investigate them.

Print books

Jim Nash

Jim Nash The Beginning
Gun Crazy
Gun Crazy 2
Gun Crazy 3
Fallen Angels
Last Stop to Nowhere
Revenge is Justice
Escape / Forget Me Not
Wedding Bell Blues / Breakdown
Mexico Time
No Free Ride / Gone
LOBO
Stealing America
Blame It on Djibouti
No Escape
Trouble in Paradise
Nash & Delaney Collide

Harry Delaney Adventures

Dead Reckoning
Lie Cheat Steal
Uncharted
Go-Around
Sand Storm
Harry Delaney Collection

Frank Ross Biker Tales

No Way Out
Bad Girls
Bank Robber Dames

Other

The Last President

Jim Nash Read Order

Marina Mystery
Twisted Sisters
Sleeping with a .45
Pirate Cay
Thrill Kill Jill
Greetings From Key West
Lost Paradise
No Angels
Mexico Gamble
No Picnic
Fallen Angels
Vendetta
A Girl's Best Friend
Dead End
No Harbor
Dog Days
Dead End
No Harbor
Dog Days

Startup Blues
Last Stop to Nowhere
Revenge is Justice
Escape
Wedding Bell Blues
Breakdown
Little Girl Lost
Forget Me Not
All The Glitter
Mexico Time
Partners in Crime
Shop Till You Drop
LOBO
No Free Ride
Gone
Stealing America
Blame It on Djibouti
No Escape
Trouble in Paradise

SEASONAL

Trick or Treat
Helping Santa

JIM NASH INVESTIGATES

Snap Brim Fedora Caper
The Lady in White
The Lady in Yellow

Sleeping with a .45 - 84

Detective Nash has a couple of problems, and they involve dead bodies. As if that wasn't enough, someone is trying to kill him, and the killer's methods aren't very inventive. In fact, they're pretty old-fashioned.

Pirate Cay - 138

Jim Nash and companion Zelda are bound for a long-awaited vacation in the Florida Keys. When he finally bothers to checks his messages, he discovers an old flame needs his help. After a brief consult with the new female in his life, Jim heads west to Panama Crossing, where he becomes embroiled in the rough seas and rocky shores of drugs, guns and money.

MARINA MYSTERY

I became involved in the investigation completely by accident. The murder case I was working on crossed paths with high-class hookers hanging out at marinas. They were there to service the boats that arrived and departed.

Boats was probably a misnomer. In fact, I knew it was. These weren't boats by any stretch. They were high-end yachts. Floating residences. Homes away from homes. Some were big enough to come with butlers and chefs when the money didn't matter and the owner thought he might make an impression on someone else with their own butlers and chefs. Whatever. It was all past my retirement income.

Initially, I figured there couldn't be much of a market for prostitutes click-clacking their way up and down the yacht club docks on unsteady feet dressed in high heels. Even if there was, surely these guys brought their own hookers with them. How else did all the good-looking women in bikinis figure into the equation?

And then I learned that boat-owning, horny millionaires wanted nothing more than to escape wives and families and business pressures. Some didn't want to set sail out of the harbor.

That was news to me. It shouldn't have been. Perhaps it was only me, but I figured that if a man was wealthy enough to own a sailboat or a yacht, that ought to be escape enough. It would be for me. But then, I was a simple S.O.B. when it came to things like that.

And I knew I'd never be in that position. Well, maybe with a canoe one day and missing paddles the next. I knew my limits, too.

The problem I had was tying the hooker discovered in the water to the marina and one or more of its wealthy denizens. If I knew one thing for certain, it was that a rich lawyer—or more likely, an entire firm of lawyers—would be on call at the drop of a hat.

In this case, at the drop of a prostitute's underpants. The best I could hope for would be a few interviews where everyone said they knew nothing, hadn't been anywhere near the marina on the day in question, and thanks but no thanks to everything else.

Which was why I asked for a coroner to meet me. I wanted all the lead time I could get. Knowing when the woman ended up in the drink would help me narrow down the comings and goings around the marina.

If I got real lucky, someone would have security camera feed for me to look at.

Once the hookers got under sail, it was only natural that, along with everything else, drugs got to sail away, too. It was supposed to be classy. It was anything but. Usually, the coke-starved individuals got too much of a good thing. Bodies ended up dumped into the ocean.

It wasn't often, but occasionally, dead hookers defied the odds and drifted ashore, thanks to stoned boat owners who were too stupid to see where they were anchored too close to shore. That's when I got called in to figure out what went wrong. Which is why I got involved in this marina thing.

High-class hookers don't look any different from low-class hookers. With one exception. They seemed to dress a little better and carry more expensive purses. And they were younger—at least until the drugs got to them and took over.

Then, they looked like and behaved like addicted street hookers everywhere.

Call me prejudiced if you want. I don't mind. When you've got my experience, prejudice goes along with the job.

So where was I? Oh yeah, I'm on this floating hooker thing that got fished out of the harbor near the marina. I had to meet up with the coroner somewhere. I figured I'd kill time looking at the nice shiny boats in the marina while the coroner got here, since that's all I could afford to do.

Looking is cheap.

Sort of like hookers, until you had to pay up for services rendered.

The floating hooker had no purse. No pockets. No bra. No panties. She didn't have any cash on her, either. Unless she had it tucked away somewhere private. In that case, it wasn't my job to look for it. It was up to the coroner.

That's when I got a first look at Allie.

I'd heard about her, of course. Well-qualified and experienced, she was slowly making a name for herself in the city's M.E. office. Some of the detectives on the force liked her no-bullshit attitude when it came to investigating. A few more didn't like it when a woman shot their pet theories to-hell-and-gone with unassailable facts.

They probably didn't like that she was tall, either. With long, dark hair and eyes to go along with the hair and the tall. Slim, but not flat, if you get my drift. Personally, I didn't mind as soon as my eyes found her.

I enjoyed having nice things to look at besides boats. It made my day go appreciably better. And faster. Even if I was stuck with a naked, floating hooker with bad teeth and track-marks running up one of her arms and down the other.

She didn't have a ring. Allie, that is, not the floating hooker. That's the first thing I looked for these days. I never used to.

Until I had to start.

One too many times I'd come up with a married woman's husband filing a complaint with the department. Ever since the last one knocked the wind out of me because I fell in love with the woman, I looked for rings.

No ring was good.

The woman on the end of the wharf with the long hair and the skirt blowing in the wind was good, too. I caught a look before she caught her skirt. Nice.

She didn't even blush.

"You the coroner I've been hearing so much about?" I asked.

"I guess. Whatever that means. I'm Allie Sands." She held out a hand.

"Jim Nash. I'd shake, but I've got a naked hooker on the end of my line and I don't want her to get away. You're not dressed for fishing. I've got coveralls in my car if you want a pair," I offered.

"Thanks. I'll take you up on that. I was on a day off when I got the text," she volunteered.

I pulled out the keys and tossed them. She did a one-handed catch. The other kept busy holding down her dress in the wind coming off the water. She already knew I had hungry eyes.

"Jim Nash. Do I know that name? It sounds familiar."

Oh-oh. Once again my reputation preceded me. "Nah. I'm one of the quiet ones around these parts. Head down. Keep my mouth shut. Do my job. Go home and try to live a different life until I have to punch in again."

"It'll come to me. It always does," she said.

That's what I was afraid of, but you never know. Just maybe what comes to her wouldn't be all bad.

The body floated close to the wharf. It bobbed up and down like a cork in what little swell made it past the breakwater and between the huge docks.

"It looks like the fishing wasn't so good for someone. What have you got for me?"

"Probably a dead hooker. Rotten teeth. No clothes. No purse. Drug addict by the look of her arms. Can't tell her age. Probably tossed overboard when she overdosed. Or she fell overboard and nobody cared. Or pushed overboard just to watch her drown."

"Nice crowd you hang with. You get nightmares often?" she asked.

"Only when I sleep alone. You?"

"Not much bothers me. It's all part of the job. Where are those coveralls you handed me that line about?"

I tied off the small boat and the hooker on the end of the rope and climbed the steps to the dock. "Follow me."

She handed back the keys. I led her to my car and opened the trunk. I could tell Allie had moxie right off the bat. By the time I straightened up, she had dropped her dress, slipped out of her blouse, and was bending over to reach in for the coveralls.

I had a double good look when she bent over again to pull them on.

"Thanks. I needed that. Dead hookers will do that to a man sometimes."

"You're welcome. What do you like to do when you're not staring at an ME's ass?"

"Well, for starters, I don't stare at all of them." If she was going to ask me out on a date, that was a new one on me. Normally, I didn't like to associate with cops after work. It was too depressing in the dark bars they hung out in. A coroner, on the other hand, would definitely be a step up.

Still, I ignored the question. I'd have to think about it. Just because a woman on a dock, in plain sight, gets undressed in front of me in broad daylight, didn't make me an easy date.

To put it another way, I was no pushover.

Yeah, right.

"Is no one coming to help you?" I asked.

"No. We're short staffed plus it's the weekend. Give me a hand with the bag and tag, will you? Have you got gloves?"

"Have I got gloves. Let's go and get it done," I told her.

I helped Allie slide the slippery, heavy corpse out of the water. Together, we lifted the poor woman onto the wharf.

"Help me roll her on her back, would you?" she asked.

We flipped her for a better look. She did a quick inspection of the rest of her. Looked into multiple orifices. Didn't find anything.

Except teeth. The girl had all of her teeth. They were good, too. Not like I first thought.

"She's young. Pretty good looking before spending all that time in the water, too."

"How long?" I wanted to know, but I already knew she couldn't answer definitively until she got her on the block.

"A day. Two max. Maybe. Maybe not."

I wasn't surprised. The body had been sitting in saltwater. "Thanks for the solid answer. It'll make my investigation go that much smoother." I smiled at her anyway, to let her know I wasn't serious.

I helped tuck the body into the black bag. She zipped it shut with a satisfying sound.

"Look. You know as well as I do I'm going to have to get her back to the office to do the proper work. Cut me some slack."

I knew. In fact, I knew so well I was grinning at her like a man that just caught the biggest fish of his life. Except, I'd never been fishing. Ever. "In that case, I'll see you back at the office, Allie Sands."

I opened the car door.

"Wait. What about my dress?"

I knew she'd be there until the wagon arrived. She'd have to wait with the body. "What about it? You looked pretty good to me without it."

That got her blushing.

"I'll bring it with me—if I don't end up putting it under my pillow for luck," I said.

"If you put it under your pillow, keep it. I wouldn't want to rob you of happy times between the sheets."

She was a smartass, too. I liked that about her right off.

All I had to do was try to figure out if the woman in the water had anything to do with the murder on the yacht tied up in the harbor. The yacht belonged to a venture capitalist. I was looking to him for more information.

Greg Vice—yeah, I know—was found on his yacht in this very marina. Someone had stuck a needle in his arm, pushed the plunger down all the way, and didn't' bother to take the time to pull it out.

Or maybe he did it himself.

Whoever he had on the boat with him was long gone. One, none, or a hundred, I had no idea. The marina's security cameras were out with a failed server. No backup available.

Which is usually par for the course. They all cheap out on the backups once they figure out the bill of goods sold them on the surveillance system.

The night watchman, the day watchman, and the marina regulars saw nothing. It wouldn't be good for business if they gave up all of their secrets, anyway. Even I knew that.

So I was at a dead end.

The only viable solution staring me in the face was that of a public pissing contest Greg Vice got into with another VC—venture capitalist—over the funding and purchase of a resort property down south. Their deal started out as a partnership. Then one or the other, depending on which story one believed, started taking money from the accounts on the sly.

Bank statements said they were both guilty of that part of it. It was probably standard fare if one wasn't shy about those things. By the look of it, neither was shy. By the look of it, it was a tossup who would get murdered first over that kind of money. As it turned out, it was Greg Vice.

Yeah. I know. That name again. But I couldn't hold it against the man that Vice liked vice. And vice versa.

Or that a man with two first names was the prime suspect.

* * *

Robert George—another one with two first names—was a self-made man. By the time he hit his early twenties, he'd made his millions from a couple of smartphone apps. Being a bit of a dinosaur with a flip phone myself, I didn't hold it against him. That he hadn't turned into a complete asshole impressed me, too.

I mean, really, when you've made your first million at such a young age and didn't turn into an instant asshole, there was something to be said for your upbringing. And your family.

I met them all when I stopped by the mansion they shared in an upscale neighborhood. Robert had purchased the property, complete with a second house on the enormous lot. He lived in the smaller house.

The rest of the brood lived in the main house. They included a mother, a father, and two sisters. I met the sisters when they answered the door in stereo. The pair of them took turns flirting.

I decided on the spot if I was ever given the chance, I'd tag-team them. It seemed as though they agreed with my decision. When one left to get the parents, the other tried to sit in my lap while I was standing up. "I'm sorry, but you're going to have to wait for your sister before anything happens," I volunteered.

"No problem. That can be arranged," sister number two said.

Footsteps interrupted what was turning into a mutual admiration society of two. All I needed was sister number two, and I'd be in heaven. Then mom and dad showed up to the party.

"You must be Mr. and Mrs. George. I'd Detective Nash. I'm here investigating a murder on a yacht in the marina."

"That's horrible. Do you have a suspect yet?" they wanted to know.

Obviously, these two hadn't watched many TV detective shows. "No, but we're working a couple of angles."

"We don't own a boat, but our son does. My husband and I get seasick, so we've only been out once."

"We're interviewing everyone who has a boat tied up at the marina," I explained. "Is he here now?"

"He lives in the smaller house in the back. Girls, why don't you take Detective Nash to see your brother?"

I left a card. "Call me if you remember anything."

The sisters walked me to the door. It closed behind us and they surrounded me on the walk to the rear of the mansion.

"Don't I get a card?" sister one asked.

I fished for one. The dishwater blond put it in the back pocket of her cutoffs.

"Where's mine?" sister two asked.

I reached for another and watched as bleach blonde tucked her card into ample cleavage. I wondered if there might be a cell phone in there somewhere, too.

There was definitely room.

The sisters deposited me at the door to the house.

"So long, detective. We'll see you later."

It was all I could do to keep my jaw from dropping, and it wasn't at the long legs and fine rear ends in retreat.

I looked up and down and side to side. If this was what mom and dad called a small house, I sure couldn't tell. Judging by mansion number two, the venture capital business looked to be doing pretty well. I punched the button and waited. I looked hopefully in the direction the sisters had disappeared. They were nowhere to be found.

The door opened to a man in his mid-twenties. Tall, about six-three. Blond hair to match his sisters—although at least one of the sisters was bottled. I expected a kid with too much money who knew it. What I found was an entirely different story.

"I'm Detective Nash. Are you Robert George?" I asked.

"I am. Can I help you?"

"Possibly. May I come in?" I was expecting to ask the questions from outside the door. George surprised me by inviting me in. I followed him into the massive foyer.

"Do you live here alone?"

High-pitched laughter announced the arrival of the sisters. I thought they had beaten a too-hasty retreat. I should have known better.

"He's mostly alone," sister one said. "Except for the times he stacks them up like cord-wood upstairs."

Robert blushed somewhat painfully at the dig. "Ignore them. They're trouble."

Somehow, I already knew that. I figured it was going to be a matter of how soon and how much.

"Come on, you two," he called to them. "Cut me some slack. The detective wants to ask me some questions. I don't need you putting words in my mouth in front of him."

Doors closed. We were alone.

"You probably know why I'm here, but I'm going to tell you anyway."

News headlines notwithstanding, I explained about finding Greg Vice dead on his boat in the marina. I didn't mention anything about the needle in his arm or the empty wine glasses that were been scrubbed clean. Security cams had images of Robert George and his car in the lot earlier in the day. They showed him entering the building and proceeding to the restaurant.

That's where the footage ended, and everything went dead, camera-wise.

"Can you tell me what transpired after you walked into the building?" I asked.

"I had a meeting scheduled with Greg. We were on the verge of an agreement on the southern property regarding how we'd split the proceeds.

You know, whether we would sell it, or go ahead with the construction. Once we finalized verbally, we'd be leaving it to our respective representatives to put it on paper."

"Your lawyers. Was the meeting cordial?"

"Yes, our lawyers. At the start, the meeting was friendly. But toward the end, with Greg drinking his lunch the entire time, it started to fall apart."

"How so?" I asked.

"Greg fell back to his position that I screwed him out of the property. That wasn't true. His name was still on the deed."

"Why do you think he believed that?"

"I don't know, but he was pretty adamant about it. You can ask the servers. I don't know whether it was his lawyers or his partners causing the trouble. I hoped it wouldn't be my problem, but obviously, with him dead, it's become a major problem."

"Where did you go when you left the restaurant?" I asked.

"I went straight to my office."

"Did anyone see you?"

"Not that I recall. It was Saturday, remember?"

I thanked the man for his time and departed. Somehow, I managed to avoid the sisters.

I folded Allie's skirt and blouse in a paper evidence bag and headed out to the ME's office. On the way, I tried to put it all together, but it was too early. Even so, there was motive. Hundreds of millions of dollars of motive.

Opportunity was another matter. No one could have known that the security cams would be out of service around the entire marina complex. George couldn't possibly have known about the outage.

Hell, half the staff, including the security guards, didn't know about the failure. They were dumb enough to think that if they could see a picture on a monitor the system was recording it.

On the way to the ME facility, I turned into the marina. A little fraternization wouldn't hurt when it came time to ask more questions. Imagine the surprise when I spied the sisters at the bar, yukking it up and flirting with the bartender.

I watched for a few from the doorway. On the spur of the moment, I decided to join them. I knew better. I always did. I always ignored the knowing better part, sometimes much to my dismay. This would probably turn out to be one of those times.

It was after quitting time, though. I was my own boss now.

Number one elbowed number two. She turned around to face her sister and almost fell off the stool. "Well. Look what we have here. It's a detective."

"In that case, since my reputation precedes me, I won't need to show a badge," I said with a smile. That got me a smile and a giggle.

"Do you think we should call 911, or should we just tie him up and take him home?"

"Our house, or his?" number one wanted to know.

"Let's go to his. Come on, detective man. It's now or never."

It was an easy choice.

The women piled into the unmarked car, flipped on the lights and siren, and generally screwed around all the way to my place. It was a tossup as to who was the nuttier of the pair. By the time I got them upstairs and quieted down, I decided all three of us were crazy.

Morning couldn't come soon enough. When it did, it blossomed into someone pounding on the door at a pace that matched the pounding in my head. I struggled to untangle from the pile of female parts and managed to shove them out of the way.

Normally, I'm the kind of guy that likes to see a woman at my door any time of the day. Today was an entirely different matter, because when I eventually made my way and opened it, it turned out to be Allie on the outside. Looking in.

"Nice pants. Who does your laundry?"

I knew by the smile and the cups of coffee in each hand she was happy to be here. And I was happy to see her until I was reminded of what I had in my bedroom.

"Detective Jim, are you ever coming back? It's not time for work yet."

Allie's smiling face turned to one of curiosity. Thankfully, she didn't toss the coffee.

"Is this a bad time?" she wanted to know.

"Well—" I hesitated.

The women pushed past both of us and headed down the staircase. At least they were dressed. "So long, Detective Jim. It's been a slice. We'll call you."

I shrugged and stepped back, not sure if that deserved a comment.

"Obviously you didn't hear me. Is this a bad time?" Allie repeated.

I considered for only a split second. "Not any more. Come on in."

I almost fell over when she did. I turned around and went in search of something to wear.

Allie motioned with the coffee. "You look like you could use some of this."

I took a cup. "Yes I could. Thank you. Now if you'll give me a couple, I'll be right back."

I danced through the shower in record time, dried, dressed, smoothed the sheets and made the bed. Damned if the last two people out of it hadn't bothered.

"All right. I feel presentable now," I announced.

"You don't look it," she said.

"Thanks. You look great. To what do I owe the honor of your drive-by so early in the day?"

Allie didn't answer right away. She was busy looking around, taking the place in. I had to admit, there wasn't much to take in. I lived a spartan life. My job was my home—at least, up to now, it had been.

I took a better look at this woman who had the balls to show up uninvited, bearing coffee gifts. Hell, she deserved a second look. She made everything in my place look cheap, and she wasn't even wearing a little black dress. The dark slacks and the white blouse hid just enough to make a man wonder what she might be covering up.

Since I was a man, I wondered, even though I had a partial look the day before.

"By the way, the evidence bag was a nice touch. Tacky, but nice."

"I figured you wouldn't want me walking around your office with your clothes in my hands. It was the best I could do on such short notice."

"Thanks for that bit of discretion. Now I remember the name."

Oh-oh. Here it comes.

"All the women in the building warned me about you when I first started," Allie admitted.

That was a strange one. I never put the moves on any of them that I could remember.

"What did they say?" I was curious now.

"Two words."

I marveled at the fact. "Only two?"

"Yes. Stay. Away."

"All the women said that?" I wanted to know.

"Pretty much."

"Yet here you are."

"I have to be a fool for punishment," she admitted.

I took a slug of cold coffee. "Only if you keep coming back. There's a little place across the street—"

"That's where I got the coffee."

We walked across, accompanied by the noise of her heels click-clacking on asphalt. I quite enjoyed the sound. It wasn't coming from a stripper's Lucite heels nor a hooker's screw-me pumps, two things I was quite familiar with thanks to my last case.

"You were going to tell me what you were doing on my side of town so early."

We settled in to a two-top to wait for our coffee.

"It's about the water in your floating dead hooker's lungs."

Allie looked pretty sure of herself. Hell, she ought to. From what I had been told when I began asking, she was one sharp cookie.

"There's no doubt. The water in her lungs is sea water."

Damn. She even knew what I was thinking, and we had only just met. Perhaps she had a natural skepticism.

"So that means—"

"Yes," she interrupted. "Whether she fell or was pushed off the boat while still alive is yet to be determined. I have to go back and take another look at all of it."

Accidental drowning? Not likely. When a hooker showed up, the last thing she would think about would be taking a swim. Thrown off the boat would be more like it. Falling off in a drug-induced coma wouldn't be far off the mark, either.

Allie wiped away the donut sugar lingering on her lips with a napkin. I thought it was the cutest thing I'd ever seen. Up to now, I hadn't been paying attention. Normally, by now, I'd have looked.

So I did.

The sun had left a light outline where a wedding band once had been. A thick one, judging by the width. I thanked the sun god and pretended not to notice. Instead, I filed it away.

"Anything else about the case?"

So she was just separated or divorced. What else could there be? Kids? I didn't think so, but you could never tell for sure. I looked at her and pretended to listen.

"An addict. Track marks up and down both arms and on the feet. You already noticed that. Bruises around the neck, possibly acquired during an attempted strangling. Not enough that it was the cause of death.

"Do you have a cause?" I asked.

I thought I'd like to make her a cause, although I'm almost certain she'd have something to say about that. I let her go on.

"Not yet. We're waiting for toxicology. That'll tell us if it was a drug overdose that contributed to the drowning."

"So it could have been an OD, intentional or otherwise."

"Perhaps. Like I said, we're waiting on results."

"So there's no chance she was moved?" I thought about that for a minute.

"She couldn't have fallen into a salt-water pool, could she? And then moved? Where are you parked?"

"In the alley. Why?"

She probably didn't want to be seen anywhere near my place. I couldn't blame her. "Leave it there and come with me." She didn't ask where we were going. Instead, she got in, sat down and shut up.

The more time I spent with her, the more I liked her.

I drove and asked the questions. She was a midwest girl. Sensible until it came time to decide on a career. She chose modeling for a while, until she figured out it was a nowhere job to a nowhere end. Drugs and bulimia scared her off that.

She ended up in university with a part-time summer job digging graves to help pay the bills. She considered stripping. Said she had the body for it, but decided against that, too, even though she was desperate for cash.

I had to agree she had the body for it. After all, I'd seen it before a pair of coveralls blinded me.

It all worked out when she graduated. And then she went back for more. Seven years more.

I had to admire the balls to do that when you're broke. But she had paid it all off, and then some. Now she was in the market for a house.

"We're here," I announced as I turned into the George driveway. "Come in with me. I'll distract the good-time girls while you get a sample. Have you got a vial or something?"

"I've got a plastic bag. I can tell them I'm looking for goldfish. Wait, the good-time girls? You don't mean—" She looked at me and raised an eyebrow.

"The pool is behind the big house," I told her. I caught her looking up at the house behind the gate.

"Not that one. It's the one behind it. You can sample that pool on the way out."

"Holy shit."

"Yeah. That'd be the guy to bag if you wanted someone to buy your house for you."

"No thanks. I want to do that on my own," Allie said. "I have principles."

She obviously knew I didn't. I had been the one with the nerve to drag her to the home of the twisted sisters with which I'd become entangled the night before. The very same ones that greeted her at my door.

"Jim. You came back," sister one said. The two women scurrying toward me slowed in lockstep when they got a look at Allie.

"Oh." Scowls replaced grins. "You brought her."

I didn't need to be an expert with women to know that wasn't a good sign.

Allie ignored the snark and walked past the sisters without giving them so much as a look. At the pool, she bent with the baggie to take a sample. It didn't go well.

By the time I helped her out, she had enough of a sample to set aside. She rushed up to sister number one. A roundhouse punch knocked the girl into the pool. She was fast on track for number two by the time I managed to get an arm around her and carry her off. Her feet kept moving.

"Come on, champ. I have coveralls in the trunk just for you."

Just like last time, she stripped down and donned the outfit. "This is getting to be a habit. I'm sorry I don't have dry underwear for you."

"There's not one chance in hell I'll be putting on any underwear you had in there. I'd be worried all day where it came from."

TouchŽ. She had me.

"I don't think you should go back to the office looking like that for a second day. There's a laundromat across from my place—"

"It's almost like you planned it this time," she said past a smile.

If only I could be so lucky.

I found a clean bathrobe for Allie and trundled across the street with the laundry. I stopped at the bakery for fresh coffee and donuts. By the time I returned, Allie had disappeared.

"What the hell are you doing in there?"

A mess of bedding lay piled at the foot of the bed. Obviously, she'd gone through the place to find clean sheets.

"I didn't get any sleep last night. Now take those downstairs. Before you bring them back up here, make certain they're clean, or I'm never coming back," she announced.

And that, as they say, was that. I disappeared for a couple of hours. I came back with fresh laundry. I was forced to watch the woman change again. This time, it was different.

She got naked. So did I.

Perhaps she had misheard all the women in her office.

The fridge door opened and slammed shut in a second. "There's nothing to eat," Allie announced.

"I don't want to sound like I'm making excuses, but had I known you were coming, I'd have baked a cake." That wasn't a lie. I damned well would have for this one.

"Yes, well, don't expect me on a regular basis. Keep the cakes to a minimum or they'll go stale." Allie stood in the door, her fine figure outlined by the light streaming in from the living room. She had a great body to go along with everything else about her.

"Don't be such a showoff and come back here." I was practically begging.

"Not on your life. I'm sticking with what the women at the office said."

"It's too late for that. When you show up, it's definitely not staying away." There was no way I was confused about that.

"Where's my clothes?" she asked.

"Why don't I get up and help you look?"

"You're already up," she said. "Why don't I get back in bed instead?"

"Make up your mind, why don't you?"

"No. It's my job as a woman to keep you unbalanced."

"Then you're certainly doing a good job of that, let me tell you." It was true. There was no sense in denying the obvious.

"Now let's get going. And don't forget to go in your car. If you ask me for a ride, I won't be able to say no. I wouldn't want to start any rumors after just being introduced to you."

"In that case, you definitely need to know you can't expect this on a regular basis." Allie did a bounce and a pirouette and headed for the living room. "Come on, Jim. Rise and shine—and not the way you want to rise and shine."

We took our separate ways to our respective offices with promises to stay in touch. I'd heard that one more than a time or two. It was code for don't call me, I'll call you.

So I didn't.

Instead, I put everything into the case and still came up with nothing. I got an email from Allie. It confirmed that the water in the hooker's lungs wasn't from the George pool she'd taken the header into.

At the end of the day, I went home. I would have slept like the dead but for the scent of the woman still in my bed. She kept me awake well into the morning.

Which was why I heard someone walking on my tar-paper and gravel roof at three a.m.

The only other people in the place were at the opposite end of the strip mall. They ran a dog grooming business. The suite I was in was an afterthought by the owner of the building. He thought having an apartment on the roof would keep problems away.

It did, too. But not tonight, apparently. I kept an ear pealed and went for my pistol and badge. One can't be too careful these days.

The Molotov cocktail crashed through the window right in front of me. In a split second I returned it through the same broken glass. It landed with a shattering sound and a thump. Gasoline fumes ignited in a deep orange glow.

I knew for sure I'd never hear the end of this one. Out the window, my precinct car burned brightly. I'd set fire to my own car.

I dialed 911 and waited for the verbal abuse I knew would be coming my way in short order.

When the smoke cleared, I took a taxi to the precinct. Like good cops everywhere, someone had radioed ahead. A ceremonial guard was formed along the street to herald my arrival on foot. I gave my impression of a royal wave and climbed the steps. At the top, I turned and made them all think I was about to give a speech.

Instead, I rushed into the building, only to be greeted by more applause and laughter. I'd be a long time living down the fact that I set fire to my own cop car. Even Allie got in on the deal. Smartypants had left a message volunteering to do forensics on the car.

By the time I filed my preliminary report and landed it on the captain's desk, I was ready to approach the auto pool. I ended up with a brandnew black and white, complete with Christmas tree.

Right off, I figured I'd stalk Allie. I was hoping the toxicology report might be in. On the way, I picked up a couple of coffees and headed over. Somehow, the questioning glances from the women in the office didn't appear. I guess no one knew about us yet.

"Is it in yet?"

"You're not that well-endowed. If I feel anything, I'll let you know," she grinned.

I snickered before handing over a coffee. I settled into a chair across from her desk for the long haul.

"It should be here any minute," she admitted.

"Did we miss anything on the body? Tattoos? Scars? Anything?

"No. But there were signs they tied her up. Nautical rope judging by the pattern."

"So she was on board a boat."

"More than likely," she agreed. "Any of a hundred. Or more. There were small amounts of teak wood and some fiberglass in one of the cuts. A nice light blue."

"Which only narrows it down by half," I had to admit.

"You're right. She most likely wouldn't have got that in a pool."

"She wasn't moved and dumped. Here's what we've got so far. A dead hooker swimming in the bay. Drowned overdosed. By who or what we don't know. Carted out or fell out of a boat. Free to swim with the fishes and wash back and forth with the tide."

"That sounds about right to me. Did you bring donuts?"

I looked around before replying. "Judging by what I saw last night—"

"Fat chance."

I droned on. "Maybe what we have are two entirely different crimes. If there's nothing to put the two together. And no, I didn't bring you donuts. I'm concerned about spoiling your girlish figure.

She grinned. "It's nice to know you were thinking about me, at least."

I was thinking about her, all right. I was thinking about what I would have to do to get her back in my bed sooner rather than later.

I didn't know it when I dialed 911 to report the burning car in my front yard, but homicide got busy picking up Robert George. He ended up charged with the murder of Greg Vice, his business partner in the resort deal. People higher up the chain of command obviously knew more than I did.

From what I could tell, the evidence was circumstantial. They wanted to send a message and put the fear of the lord into him. All the better if it would scare a confession out of the man, too.

Robert asked to see me, rather than call an attorney. That was a new one on me. I gave him the benefit of the doubt, checked my firearm at the door and made the walk to his holding cell.

Disheveled, stripped of belt and tie and shoelaces, he looked beaten. He was nothing like the man I saw in the million-dollar residence. "Have your folks been to see you yet?"

"Not yet. They're on the way."

"What about the two crazies?" I wanted to know.

"They left town for a trip up north to the Hamptons."

"Fly or drive?"

"They chartered," he admitted.

Of course. When you've got access to money, why fly commercial? It seemed strange that they got out of town just as Robert was arrested. I'd need to think some more on that.

"You might not get out on bail, you know."

"I know. But the evidence is circumstantial. Perhaps the judge will take that into account."

"Is there anything you can tell me—even the craziest thing—about your partner? Anything at all? Even if it doesn't seem related."

He thought briefly.

"Greg used to be in electronics. High end, top secret stuff used in espionage. Cameras. Transmitters. Long-life miniature batteries to power it."

My wheels started to turn. "Do you think he might have installed something like that on his yacht?"

"It's possible. He liked to put together videos of the better parties on the boat. Perhaps that's how he got the footage to use."

Well damn. Now I had an excuse to tear apart a yacht. To cover all the bases, I went for a warrant, and in three hours, I had all the paper I needed. On the spur of the moment, I decided to see if Allie might be available to help. I should have known better when she cast a glance in the direction of my new black and white.

"Nice ride. Where's the ticket book and what's your quota?"

"For your information, I haven't been demoted. This is a loaner. I've been warned if I damage it in any way, I'll never get another until the day I retire. I'll be using my own car until then."

I grinned, turned on the lights and siren, and left rubber at the light. I should have known no one would stop. I made it through the intersection, but not before seeing a minor traffic pile-up in the rearview.

I couldn't be bothered to call it in. I knew better.

I picked up a pass-key to get us through the gates at the marina and headed for Greg Vice's yacht. Water slapped against the side. The yacht club flag shifted about in the light wind. Mid-morning sun danced off the water. It was peaceful.

"Too bad you didn't bring your bathing suit. We could party down and see what showed up to participate."

"I'm not playing lot lizard just so you can get a free look," Allie informed me. "If you want to see more of me, you'll have to buy me dinner."

"You keep forgetting. You already showed me everything there is. How does Chinese sound?" I asked.

"Not everything. And it's my favorite." Not everything? What did I miss? "Grab a pair of gloves and let's get started."

We spent a couple of hours tossing the boat. We came up with nothing. Nada.

"Let's do it again." We were another hour into it and was still nothing.

"I can't believe this," Allie said. "Are you sure he had cameras on this thing?"

"No," I had to admit. "But there is a chance, considering how he made his money."

"How small could they be?"

The sun dancing on the water caught on a bit of glass to light it up. I took a closer look. Sure enough. I took out my knife and cut through the teak frame. "Damn. Take a look at this."

"Now we know what we're looking for, at least."

It took us three tries. We came up with two dozen of the things. Now all we needed was a recorder. With a miniature power pack, something like that could be anywhere.

"I'm thinking that it wouldn't be anywhere near the engine to avoid electrical interference. Not by the nav gear, either. Or the radar."

"What does that leave us with, besides the rest of the boat?"

"Grab my flashlight and take a look in the bow. It's far enough away to be protected from any of that."

Allie was back in ten minutes, with a sweat sheen and a dirty face. She'd tied the arms of her coveralls around her waist, revealing the perspiration soaking through her sheer blouse.

"You're hot once you get a little dirt under the fingernails," I told her.

"If you want to see what I've got, you'd better be nice to me or else," she insisted.

"Or else what?" I wanted to know.

"Or else you'll be wishing you still had my dress to put under your pillow to help you sleep and dream." She wasn't smiling.

"Have you got anything that will play this?" She held up what looked like a battery pack and another equally small box.

I think she already knew better. "Are you kidding me? You've already seen everything I have, including the empty fridge."

"Then we better head to my place."

"Well I'll be damned." I wasn't certain what I was looking at, but I knew it was the evidence I needed to get an innocent man out of jail.

"Yes, you will be damned. I'll damn you to eternity if you ever sleep with those twins again," Allie said.

"That's not what I was talking about," I wanted her to know. Maybe deep down I was thinking about it.

"I was the one talking about it," she said. Allie resumed loading files from the high-speed memory card.

"Look at that," she said, as she brought up the file I needed on screen.

"I'd say we just solved the case. Speaking of which, do you have a warrant?" she asked.

"A warrant? What the hell is a warrant and why would I need one?"

Allie's jaw dropped, and I pretended to pat my pockets as though looking for one. I fished it out. I didn't want her to think I'd taken her on an illegal goose chase. "Yes, I have a warrant."

"That's good enough for me. Now we need to get those disk drives into the proper hands."

"The guys are going to have to go through that boat again in case there's something we missed," I said.

I was happy. The recorded evidence cleared Robert George. It also cleared up how a dead hooker floating in the ocean had ended up that way.

"We should celebrate." I hoped for the best, while thinking that Allie would probably turn me down because of those damned twisted sisters.

"What do you have in mind?" she asked, instead.

"I know a great little hole-in-the-wall Chinese restaurant."

"In that case, why don't you pick something up and bring it over later?"

"What's the matter? Are you afraid one of the office drones who warned you about me might find out you ignored their warnings?"

"Something like that," she said.

"Would you like anything special from the menu?" I wanted to know.

"We'll see after I let you in."

I signed in the evidence. On the way out, I stopped into holding to let Robert know. He seemed to be doing pretty good, all things considered. He did even better when I let him know what I found. "It won't be long before you're out. Hang in there. You'll be all right."

"I owe you big time for this. I won't forget it," he said.

"You don't owe me anything. I'm doing what I get paid to do," I said.

"That may be true, but even so—"

I was starting to feel good about my job. Just so it didn't go to my head, I cut Robert short and left. I stopped at home, showered down, cleaned up, and passed a razor over the stubble. Clean pants, a pressed shirt and the gun tucked into my back left me feeling good.

I felt even better leaving the shirt untucked to cover everything up. Allie was younger than me. I needed every advantage I could give myself.

I shot the breeze with the owner of the restaurant while I waited for our takeout. He and his family came here twenty years ago. Eventually, he managed to save enough, and opened up his restaurant. He never looked back. You couldn't even get an American dish in the place. It was all Chinese, all the time.

Allie greeted me at her door, and I knew right away dressing up a bit had been the right thing to do. I was actually sorry I didn't do a better job.

"You clean up pretty good, girl," I had to admit when I set eyes on her. She had slipped into a nice little number that was short and sweet, and I appreciated it with my eyes.

"And so do you—for a cop."

"Gee, thanks. I think."

"What did you bring me?" she wanted to know as her eyes settled on the bag.

"Besides me, you mean?"

"No. I'm talking about food. What did you bring me to eat?"

"I'm fine, how are you would be a nice greeting," I insisted.

She ignored me and pulled the bag from my hand. I followed behind a woman in a little black number just about long enough. Dark stay-ups and pump-me shoes completed the picture.

I'd have to see about those shoes.

The stay-ups and the shoes worked themselves off. So did the little black number. We did a re-heat of the food, and all was good in my world.

"Were you able to let Robert know we got the goods for him?"

"He was relieved it was over. He promised me the world for doing what I get paid to do. I doubt that he'll come through with anything. It rarely turns out that way when they're in a hurry to forget the bad parts. In any case, I couldn't accept it anyway."

She nodded. "You're probably right about that."

"Can I set the table?"

"It's already set. Go and sit down."

Candles burned, lights went out, and we dug in.

"Finding those recordings put the icing on the cake. Who would have known there were two hookers on the yacht without them?"

"The guys will have the second woman in the back of a squad car in no time. Robert is one lucky son of a gun."

"All right then. Enough about work. Tell me everything you want me to know about you," Allie insisted.

"Ladies first."

Allie got up from the table.

"Who's doing the dishes?" I wanted to know.

"I'm not sure yet. Come with me." She didn't have to drag me into the bedroom.

"My condoms are under the bed."

"So you can reach them from the floor?"

"Sometimes," she said.

It was all good. I was happy an innocent man was proved innocent, thanks to a cop. A guilty person was nailed by the victim's own spy gear. And I had a new friend.

"I can't find the condoms." I was on my hands and knees on the floor, searching under the bed.

"That's because I keep them far enough under there that I can use not having any as an excuse to throw out whoever I want. I wouldn't want a man getting comfortable enough to move in."

"That's harsh," I had to admit.

"No. That's the way it is." Allie ran her hands over my body. "Oh, wait. It feels to me like you might be ready for another one. Why didn't you say so?"

"In that case, why don't we look under the bed together?"

TWISTED SISTERS

The call-out demanding that I do my duty came on one of those dark nights with no moon and no chance of one, given the cold drizzle accompanied by an all-enveloping dreary fog.

Weather never much hindered an investigation—beyond washing away evidence, of course. It didn't make an unpleasant task any more pleasant. And I was never happy to be dispatched to one of these, no matter the weather or the time of day.

One of these was a body on its back in a dark alley. I turned on my flashlight for a little help and a better look. Blood and two bullet holes stared back. I reached into a pocket and pulled out the gloves. I worked them on before using a hand to lift the torso only part way up. I needed a quick look without disturbing the crime scene. Using my other hand, I aimed the flashlight and discovered a hundred-dollar bill under the corpse. I allowed the body to roll back into its original position.

I used my light to sweep the ground close to the body. No shell casings. No pool of blood. The rain wasn't hard enough to wash it away. I widened the search area around the body. Nothing there, either.

It looked like the body was moved and dumped. Pump and dump, we called it. As in pumped full of lead in one place and moved to another. I squinted into the drizzle and took a quick look for cameras. Probably none. Who put cameras in a dark alley?

The overall picture was unusual, given the circumstances. It was unusual in the sense that the woman didn't look like a hooker or a drug addict or both. She was a good-looking girl. Well-dressed. Her clothes appeared to be expensive. Not too much makeup. Hair in place. No track marks on her arms when I pulled up the sleeves for a look.

The woman was young. She had a dark jacket covering up a white blouse. A couple of buttons undone on the shirt. Just enough to say maybe, not enough to say slut. My flashlight reflected a hint of sparkle winking back at me on her upper chest beneath the blouse, just above the bra.

I traced the length of her with the light and revealed a longish skirt covering most of her legs. Given the clothes, she looked kind of classy. Definitely not going for the hooker look in that outfit. I lifted her skirt and redirected the light for a better look.

Panties intact down below.

Yeah, I know. Call me a pig. I'm used to it. And I needed to know if there was a possibility the girl was assaulted before or after she was killed.

The crime scene equipment arrived. Someone handed me a coffee. I let them know I owed them one. I waited while the lights were set up and then I went back to work. The bright lights did what the taxpayers paid them to do, and I was able to get a better look.

Makeup and mascara appeared to be piled on pretty thick. It wasn't messed. Lipstick was bright and straight and not smeared. Hair neatly on top of her head and fastened with a clasp. Clean, unbroken nails with dark red polish to match her lips. Same with her toes on the foot with no shoe.

I allowed the body to roll back a second time after changing my mind about the hundred bucks. I switched my attention to search through the victim's jacket pockets. Nothing. At first glance, everything in the purse looked like it should be there. A bit of cash and change.

Her name was Candice Season. Miscellaneous business cards. One from a strip club. A dance club, they preferred to be called. A name on the back was hand-written in a girlish script.

The purse was bagged along with everything else, minus the card. The hundred under the body would have to wait on the coroner. I didn't want to chance messing something up.

"Anything interesting, Nash?" A voice in the dark beyond the lights before the body attached to it walked into the powerful glow of the lamps.

Speak of the devil. Even at oh-dark-thirty, the devil looked pretty good with the just-out-of-bed hair. The leggings didn't do a thing to diminish the woman's good looks, especially since the jacket only went as far as her waist.

"Nothing much out of the ordinary, Allie," I told her. "It looks like a pop and drop. Most likely not a robbery, though, judging by what's underneath and in the purse." The Allie was Allie Sands, M.E.

"What got you here so fast all the way from the south side?" she wanted to know.

"Somebody tripped over the body and called it in. I was having Chinese in my favorite neighborhood when I got the text." The outfit was finally going modern—or so they thought. I thought they were only keeping up, late as it was.

"How's that system working so far?" she asked.

Dispatch was testing a new method of getting investigators to serious crimes. Dinosaur that I am, I was against it at first. After more explanation and a lot of listening, three of us volunteered. So far, it had worked pretty well. Added bonus: carrying a bulky radio was eliminated. No loss. The cars all came with one, anyway.

"It's not so bad. Makes me feel trendy and cool with the younger generation." It meant being at the mercy of a cell phone, but I kind of liked it. A phone, a gun and a badge were all right by me.

"If I were you I'd go with trendy, Nash," she advised. "You look like you've been wearing those clothes for a week. That's not cool."

Yeah I was a bit of a slob in the clothes department. So sue me. I didn't spend a lot of time at home doing laundry and ironing. At least I didn't smell—as far as I knew. I didn't bother checking. "In that case, trendy it is."

I took a few minutes to watch Allie go through the motions. She'd been in the job for five years, and she proved herself repeatedly to be a thorough investigator. Nothing got past her. Not even me. We'd been involved in a relationship that ended about eighteen months ago—on good terms, as far as I was concerned.

She felt the same way, and we stayed close friends. When the other got knocked for a loop in a relationship, we'd sympathize over beer and Chinese and talk it out. Sometimes we'd spend the night, but that didn't happen often any more.

We both moved on.

I snapped a picture and checked the victim's business card for the addy of the dance club, just to be sure.

The Fontana Club was on Eighth. It was one of those streets that ran a long way through the city. If you stayed on it to the end, it would take you from high class to low class to no class—in a hurry. Not even the street lights could slow you down if you were determined. If you were fortunate, you might end up retracing your steps for another go at the run.

Most didn't. Once they were on the downhill end, they tended to stick like flies to flypaper in a poor man's summer cottage. You could thank the mortgage crisis for a lot of that. Plenty were living in their vehicles with entire families. You could thank drugs for some of it, too, but that didn't get a You're welcome, either.

The Fontana straddled the border, hovering between good taste and shithole. Closer to the shithole end, it got bought and sold regularly.

With each makeover, it would run the gamut of high low-class, biker bar, druggie hangout, low class and no class, or some semblance of order such as that.

It never attracted the type of clientele that would promote it to big-time permanently. Not even big-screen televisions and 24-hour sports channels would do that. Thus the reason for the dead televisions.

Depending on what stage it was at on its inevitable downward slide, the dancers had a long range of appearances. Trim and light and mostly tight. Not too bad. Drug-addled and downright cross and angry. Those last ended up being run by bikers.

And as always, no matter where the dance club lay in its climb or descent, there was no shortage of men who felt they had to be there.

Personally, I sometimes went there with some of the guys on a night out during a trim and tight phase, but that never lasted long. Mostly we went because of the cheap beer. And if you believed that, you'd believe anything.

The neon sign on the club's roof danced and buzzed through broken letters. A pale sheen drifted through the driver-side window on the beat-up, high-mileage, former black-and-white I was driving. The one time I got issued a new vehicle, someone took a run at me through a red light with a semi. Whoever it was won the grudge match and kept on going, like an old Timex watch.

Put me in the hospital for a week. Every damned card I got from the uniforms rubbed it in. In fact, I think some of them collected cash to buy up a collection just to drop them off at the nursing station. Which turned out to be not so bad.

The junior nurses were cute and sympathetic. The old ones just laughed. I lived down the nickname—Crash Nash—but even Allie became part of the harassment for a while. I also had a side bet with myself that the makeshift suggestion box in the coffee room got filled with thoughts on what to do with the next time-X'd black-and-white.

Happy times.

I flashed up the victim's photo on my phone and ran through what I knew about her. A younger woman, late teens, probably early twenties at most if I didn't want to believe the driver's license in her purse. Well-dressed and made up pretty good, too. Maybe a first-time dancer, or maybe so hick, she showed up for an interview in a business suit with plenty of makeup piled on for good measure.

She wasn't even a Jane Doe. Her name was Candice Season, according to her DL, her driver's license. A pretty girl with a name like that, you just knew the boys called her Candy, and they all wanted to be in season.

Jesus. Sometimes, I just can't help myself.

I took another look at the picture on the phone and shook my head. Even after five years in homicide, it still bothered me when a body turned up, no matter who or what it was. Still, she was too pretty for this place, but I guess maybe she didn't know that.

Or maybe she did.

I gave up a tired sigh, climbed out of the beater, and zig-sagged past the cars and around the puddles left by the recent rain in the uneven parking lot. There had to be some puke mixed in there too, because I could smell it over the stale beer.

I passed an open window with a foot dangling and a woman alternating screams of yes while she grunted like a pig. Or maybe it was the guy on top of her. I didn't look in. If she wasn't being taken care of, she could dial 911 and request help for all I cared.

The crowd of smokers circling around the door must have paid attention to what I was driving when I circled through the parking lot. By the time I got close, all that remained was a cloud blinking under the broken neon and the odor of marijuana. Too bad it couldn't get declared legal. That would for sure put more of us out looking for real crime.

Or maybe that was the problem.

I pushed through the door to the peeler palace and was assailed by the stink of stale beer and cigarette smoke. Dim lights illuminated a dark, low stage. Torn and bare carpet, peeling wallpaper, and missing ceiling tiles completed the picture. The dump had obviously descended to the no-class stage. It looked to me like it had been there for a while.

The dancer didn't look much better, highlighted as best she could be in the low lighting. It was obviously low for a reason. In contrast, the girls slinging the beer looked pretty good. Management would do well to hire them to do double duty as performers.

I bellied up to the bar and wedged myself between the station and the beer pulls. Even that didn't get anyone's attention. A waiter elbowed me out of the way and kept on filling the glasses she took off the bar.

"You can't be between the railings. Servers only," she told me as I got on the receiving end of another elbow.

I held the phone in front of her. "You recognize her?" I thought I saw something in her eyes until the lights on the stage blinked. The look disappeared before I could be certain.

"Never saw her before," she told me.

I switched my attention to the bartender. He didn't look all that interested, standing as he was at the far end of the bar. When I made a move in his direction, he behaved like a pig in a pen that didn't want to be slaughtered for bacon. He shifted in a hurry down to the opposite end.

I didn't have time for his shit. I chased him behind the bar and grabbed his belt. He still wouldn't look at the phone on the bar, so I pulled him close and grabbed his balls and squeezed. He took a bow and his face ended up close enough to the phone to bathe in the glow.

"Now that I've got your attention, have you ever seen her before?" In case he was far-sighted, I eased off to pull his head back, and I came up with a handful of long, greasy hair. He had to be a former hockey player. He had a mullet.

"No, man," he squealed. "She's never been in here."

"Her name's Candice Season. You sure?" I relaxed the grip just a bit to give him hope and then I squeezed one more time for good measure.

"I'm sure."

I wasn't finished. "Who's Hank?" The name written on the back of the card in the girl's purse.

"Hank?" The bartender was obviously deaf. I squeezed again, and his hearing improved right away.

"Hank's the manager. He's not here. He left for the night," the squealer said.

"When's he coming back?" I wanted to know.

"First thing in the morning, far as I know."

I planned on being here first thing in the morning to make Hank's acquaintance. Then I got a look at the woman getting ready to climb onto the stage. Instead of leaving, I found a seat at a table in front of the splash rail. I sat down, intending to do some further investigating.

I focused my energies on the stage and the dancer doing her thing. She gyrated. Squatted. Stretched. Pirouetted. Crawled. Danced. Rolled onto her back and kicked up her heels. She worked the pole like a pro. It impressed me. I didn't bother taking notes in the dim light, though. The dancer was too pretty.

Once I got done studying the bump-and-grind, I took time to concentrate on the girl's features. By the look of it, she had to be the twin of the girl I left in the alley. Either that, or the corpse I was investigating had come back to life.

I went with twin, just so I wouldn't make a fool of myself.

She had a nice little body, and she wasn't a terrible dancer. When she switched it out for the pole, she showed coordination and agility, too. A man tossed a dollar and there were no missing teeth when she smiled her thanks.

Maybe the place was moving up in the world after all.

When the set ended, I followed her to the dressing room at the side of the stage. The door guard took me for a Johnny-come-lately and let me know I should get lost if I knew what was good for me. I flashed my badge and let him know what would be good for him if he didn't let me pass.

I walked through the door and I was in a world I'd never been privy to before in my life. It was definitely a new one on me.

Half-a-dozen mirrors surrounded by high-watt bulbs greeted me in a hot, stuffy room lit up like a store-front window at dark just before Christmas. Every mirror had a woman in front of it. All were preening and prepping and readying for their next sets.

Hair and makeup and body glitter and stockings and everything else that could contribute to a dance set was being installed or adjusted. None of them appeared all that pleased a man had invaded their territory. I could tell by the dirty looks that followed me in every mirror in the joint.

That didn't bother me, though. They'd get over it.

The effect of the lighting made visible every line and wrinkle and gray hair, and I wasn't only talking about myself. That's right. Some of them were that old. At least, they looked that old from where I was standing. But then, maybe I was spoiled by Allie's good looks.

Or maybe by the last dancer I watched working the pole.

I pulled my phone and took another look at the picture of my corpse and shook it off once more. All things considered, the women in here couldn't possibly look as bad as someone who was dead. I approached the dancer I followed off the stage, but she didn't appear interested in talking. I let her have a look at my badge, and that changed everything.

"Not here. Come this way," she said.

I chased after her to a door in back of the change room. Maybe I should have been suspicious when she held the door for me. Three steps down and I ended up in an alley behind the club. The door crashed. I crashed. For the first time ever I was first through a door and flat on my back in two seconds.

When I came to, the woman was gone. I couldn't open the door to get back in, so I staggered around to the front. For my troubles, the bouncers tossed me against the brick wall like a rag doll. My head snapped back, and I was a two-time loser in the consciousness department.

Somebody must have called the fire department, because when I came to, a cute little firefighter was checking my pulse. I laid back to let her do her job, but when the smell of smoke started drifting my way, I sat up real fast.

"What the hell is going on?" I asked the cute little firefighter rendering first aid.

"The place is on fire," she informed me. "Don't worry. You're not anywhere close, Detective. I moved you. Will you be all right here?"

"Unless you plan on carrying me over the threshold after I propose, I need to find my car." I was kind of stubborn that way. I didn't need my latest ride to burn up like the first one.

She put an arm around me and helped me to my chariot, the black-and-white beater at the far end of the parking lot. It wasn't yet midnight, but this pumpkin was on his way home. "How do you know this is my car?" I asked her.

"Are you kidding? Everyone knows about your bad luck," she said. "We drove past it in the lot to get here. The captain pointed it out. If you're going to be all right, I have to go do some actual work now."

"Can I have your number in case I'm not all right?" There was always hope.

She turned, and I checked the name on the back of her turnout. "Got it." I scrawled the name in my notebook. Following the beatings, I'd never remember it. I yelled after her. "What station?"

I'm a detective. I'd track her down and give her one of the cards the boys handed out so freely after my hospital stay.

It was time to pause and regroup. I was still shaky from the shit-kicking, but not enough to keep me from figuring out something was going on with my latest case. That I didn't have a clue made me nervous, considering the beatings I was handed.

I suppose whoever wanted me dead could have ensured I'd be inhaling black smoke on the floor of the club. It didn't go that way, so maybe someone was looking out for me after all.

I had a good-looking body named Candice Season in a back alley with two holes in her chest and no signs of anything stolen. The body was definitely moved and deposited after she was killed. A card in the woman's purse led me to the Fontana where I discovered her twin dancing up a storm.

Thanks to the people who had kicked the shit out of me—twice—I still didn't know if the dead girl and the beatings were related. But why set fire to the club—if indeed it was arson?

I wasn't in that much of a daze not to recognize a woman in a firefighter's turnout gear. I came to smiling up at her. Maybe I should have gotten the message, but being the stubborn son of a bitch that I am, I didn't. Besides, it was part of my job description not to take messages. I only returned calls.

Now I had to track down a woman who disappeared and was on the run, and who might be responsible for at least some of the black and blue marks that were growing on me.

Screw it. I was exhausted, emotionally and physically. It was time to head home and crash.

The banging brought me out of what felt like a coma. I tried to hurry my way out of bed. If someone was delivering Chinese to a wounded man, I didn't want to miss out. I was slowed down by the limp, thanks to an on-the-job beating by a couple of men I would eventually track down. I limped my way to the door, whining and sniveling all the way. Damn, but sure as shit, I had a good one laid on me. It didn't keep me from opening the door without checking who was in front of it.

"Yeah?" was all I could muster. I hoped I sounded grumpy enough to send whoever it was scurrying away.

Apparently not.

"Chesterfield. Remember me?" It was a woman's voice. But there was a bright side to it, I decided.

"Vaguely. Where's your shining armor?" I wanted to know.

"You got part of it right. I'm the knight that nursed you back to health. I happened to be in the neighborhood and here I am. I came by to see how you're doing."

"I'm doing good." Apparently, that wasn't enough for Chesterfield. She needed assurance and pushed her way through the door. I almost fell down. Being the firefighter she was, she caught me on the way and propped me up.

"Yeah, I can tell by the limp I heard making its way to the door. Now let's get you back to bed. You've obviously got a concussion and you need to rest."

"How did you know where to find me?" I asked her.

"While you were out like a light, I checked your ID and found out you were a cop," she said. "I took a look at your driver's license, and here I am. Now get your ass back into bed. This time I'll stay with you until I'm certain you're all right."

She walked me into the bedroom and eased me onto the bed. I laid back like a tired dog and closed my eyes, too sleepy to care. I might have dreamed she took off her clothes and joined me. I couldn't remember for sure. In any case, she was a firefighter. I already knew she'd have a body under that uniform. I didn't need to look.

"When you have a concussion, you need someone to wake you up regularly for checkups. I'll see to it that you are."

I hated being lectured. "I recall reading something about that," I said. "Modern medical science says concussion victims—" I was too beat up to care about modern medical science. Besides, how could I refuse an offer like that?

Daylight came around and I wasn't feeling much better. My head was still pounding. Even so, I felt good enough to pull the sheet down for a better look at what I didn't care about last night.

I was right about Chesterfield and her firefighter body. The g-string she didn't take off looked to be covering up a nice, trim little runway. Her leg shifted, and I figured she was just playing at being dead, but I didn't have it in me.

I didn't have it in her, either.

"Stay right where you are, Nash. I'll be right here. I want to check up on you later."

Chesterfield rolled onto her back and slid her feet up on the sheets.

"I'll hold you to that," I told her.

"I'm counting on it," she agreed.

When I showed up at the coroner's office, Allie had the details ironed out. "High noon, sheriff. Are you working part time now?"

I told her about getting beat up at the club, and she got all concerned and shit. I didn't dare mention I had just left my personal nurse on a sleepover. It might be arguable, but just because I'm a man doesn't mean I'm as stupid as most of them. Usually.

"What have you got on the woman in the alley?" I asked.

"The woman took two in the chest from a .357. No sign of powder burns. Probably at least twelve hours before you found her."

"Any casings under the body?" I already knew there was none on the ground surrounding it.

"None. And she definitely didn't die there. There was very little blood beneath her. No evidence of rape. One tattoo on her lower back. No other marks. Nothing under the fingernails, either. She was pretty clean." Allie put the report on her desk.

"So that means they did her at a distance with no struggle."

"I'd say so," she agreed.

"That's not much to go on. Probably someone she didn't know. I'd thank you, but I don't have a reason to," I said.

"You still look like shit, by the way. Is it because of my report, or the beating someone handed you?"

"Thanks. I think."

"You're welcome."

Two phones buzzed. Allie looked at hers. I checked mine and told her I needed to attend at an address that was all too familiar.

"I have somewhere to be too, Detective Nash. Catch you later."

There was no need to check a map for the location. I knew my way home, and I didn't waste time getting there. I climbed the stairs to my walk-up with a heavy heart. I already knew what was waiting.

Chesterfield was in my bed, just the way I left her. I wasn't real happy to see her like that. She was almost floating in a vast pool of her own blood. It looked like she had lived and suffered. Whoever killed her let her bleed out.

The way everything was scattered around, someone must have come across her during a break-in and didn't want to leave a witness. It was plain he wanted to make her suffer, too.

Now I really felt like shit. The woman was only trying to be a good Samaritan. Why did she have to get dragged into the deal? I promised myself someone would suffer for this, no matter how long it took me.

I let the cops already at the crime scene do their jobs. I answered the questions as best I could. Allie would be showing up soon enough. I didn't need to be looking at my place. I needed some space.

Whoever was chasing after me didn't want me finding out anything about the body in Allie's cooler. Well, that was shot to hell now. I just experienced a personal incentive.

Two photos came up on my phone, side by side. The woman in the strip club and the murder victim were definitely twins. Candace Season was the dancer's name. Christ on mighty, but what morons name identical twins Candice and Candace, whether they were in season or not?

I was looking forward to meeting the people responsible for that travesty. I headed over to where the twins lived with their parents. A good-looking older woman greeted me when she showed up at the door with her husband in tow. I expressed my condolences, and she told me they were already notified.

I made my apologies and asked if we could sit down and talk.

Before I left, I showed the script on the back of the strip club's business card. The mother said they both wrote the same, so she wasn't any help. On the other hand, the old man blinked, and I thought his jaw was going to drop until he thought about it and changed his mind.

By the time I left, I was as confused by a case as I had ever been. At least now I had some actual photos of the two girls. And they were identical, down to the last detail. The only problem was, I was looking for an entirely different person.

The mother confirmed that the dead twin's name was, in fact, Candace. Candice must have been the dancer I saw in the club. The old girl was kind enough to show me where I could find a DNA sample for each of her daughters.

Maybe now Allie could come up with a solution.

* * *

Notwithstanding the notes I was taking, I still wasn't clear about what the hell was really going on. Twins named Candace and Candice. One dead, shot in the chest. One missing, on the run.

Could someone roll the dice and tell me where I should go and what I should do next?

I dropped the DNA samples off at the Coroner's office and high-tailed it back to the precinct. That hundred-dollar bill was nagging at me, and not in a good way. I went down to the evidence room and retrieved it from the evidence box.

I closed a finger and thumb on it and pulled it through. It didn't feel right. I held it up to a light, and it didn't look right. I grabbed an infra-red hand-held from a desk drawer and went into a broom closet to take a better look. A female uniform caught me coming out with a satisfied look and a smile on my face, and I knew I was in for it.

"Just as I thought, Nash," the uniform said. "Now I know why you never hit on me."

"That's not it at all, officer. You're not butch enough for me," I told her.

That got me the one-finger salute and the grin I was trying for. I put myself back on the street as quick as I could get there. She had a gun and knew how to use it.

At the burned-out remains of the Fontana, I crossed paths with the arson squad and one of theirs who stepped through the weakened floor. That resulted in what remained of the club's basement being roped off. He didn't get hurt, but the story he had was worth every minute of my time. What I heard said the FBI would be on its way sooner than I wanted them to show up.

I climbed down the ladder and introduced myself to a very expensive high-end color photocopier that looked to be responsible for churning out the hundred. The floor was littered with leftover loose bills scattered everywhere.

The faded pool of cleaned-up blood did it for me and now I knew where Candice Season was most likely murdered. I sniffed around and discovered a discarded shoe that was a twin to the one my victim was wearing. I still needed to know who killed her. And I needed to know where her sister disappeared to and why.

I was pretty sure someone from Allie's department could clear up the mystery of who I suspected the dried blood belonged to. All I was stuck with was a simple murder that turned into a missing person case that morphed into forgery.

Piece of cake.

I pocketed a random sample from the hundreds on the floor and climbed the ladder just as Allie arrived.

"Christ, Nash, the bodies are piling up on you. First a girl in the street. Another one in your own bed. Now a river of blood in a strip club basement. Are you sure you've been living right?" she asked.

"It was you who told me I was trendy, remember? In any case, four on the sidewalk is never allowed."

"You better hope. Do you think they're related?" she asked.

"I know they're related," I said. "I just haven't come up with the reason. Did you have time to submit the samples I sent you for testing?

"I should have the results by late tomorrow. Where are you staying?"

Allie must have heard about my place. So much for keeping secrets. "At your place. I'll see you tonight."

Two dead women. A missing person who was the exact twin of one of them. A case of forgery in the strip club where at least one twin worked and where the other one was killed. It definitely wasn't going to be all that hard to tie up the loose ends.

Right. Who said that?

I almost forgot about the dead firefighter in my bed.

I never saw the half-ton coming until it stuck itself in the side of the black-and-white beater I was herding. It put me out like a light when I banged my head against the door frame. I woke up on the same floor of the hospital where I spent time after the disgruntled semi driver took a run at me. It was like old home week with the nurses, but this time, I would only be here for a couple of hours.

Fortunately, the empty passenger side of the beater had been sturdy enough to cushion the impact. Well, that, and it took the direct hit. I took a holiday and waited where I was until the asshole in the next room came to.

The mess that was the other driver wasn't smart enough to wear his seat belt. Good thing for him I was there to keep an eye on him while he remained on life support.

I'd just have to wait and see what I could dig up on him. When he came to, I'd be digging for sure. In the meantime, how the hell would I find out who Hank, my new hospital neighbor, was working for?

M oaning led me next door to investigate. I shut the door behind me and went back to work like nothing happened. Poor Hank was out of a place to work, out of a job, and now he was out of time. I didn't have sympathy. Instead, I sat down on the fresh cast that was his new leg and turned his bed into a trampoline.

It seemed to do the trick.

My ass was showing through my hospital gown when I left the room, but Hank didn't seem to mind. He went back to sleep the moment I climbed off of him.

"Nice ass." A familiar voice. Shit. Allie.

"You say that to all the boys." I tried to make a joke out of it.

"Only the ones I care about."

"Like I said." I knew better, so I grinned, just because.

"What are you doing here?" News travels fast.

"I have the DNA results. They're definitely twins. And their prints belong to two different people."

"What do prints have to do with it?" I wanted to know.

"The DNA of identical twins is the same. Until technology takes a huge jump, at least," she said.

"So unless the missing twin shows up with a matching tramp stamp on her ass, we'll never know for sure?" I asked.

"Quite possibly. And she better not have her fingertips burned off, either," Allie said.

What little I got while babysitting my neighbor Hank in his hospital room wasn't much help. The doctors had him pumped full of too many drugs. Sitting on his broken leg helped to force him out of his stupor long enough to mumble a name. Good job, Nash, and that was all I needed.

I dressed and was on my way after saying goodbye to Allie.

The current owner of the Fontana was just another in a long line who thought they could make a go of it and ended up going broke. Only this one moved a counterfeiting operation into the basement to pay the rent. That was a no-no, especially when the dead bodies began piling up.

Christ, what was it with criminals these days? None of them had the smarts God gave to high school dropouts. Even if that was the problem, the educated ones weren't any better.

My phone buzzed, and I struggled to pull it out of my pocket. It slipped out of my hand and onto the floor. In heavy traffic, I forgot all about it and the waiting text.

I headed to my place, climbed the stairs, and reached in to grab the smoke-stained go-bag I kept by my door. I made my way to Allie's and the comfortable bed I was hoping for until the detectives finished with what I formerly called home.

I knocked and Allie opened the door and greeted me with a wide grin. "Just because you show up with a bag doesn't mean you're moving in, Nash. You'll cramp my style."

I made my way to the fridge and checked for beer. "Yeah, that's what I thought too when I stepped over the empty pizza and Chinese boxes on the way to the fridge. At least you've got beer."

I reached in, grabbed one, and popped the top. I never said no to a Sol. I developed a taste for the beer on one of my runs down the Baja years ago. Allie picked up the habit from me. "You want one?"

"Christ, Jim, give me time to close the door behind you, at least."

Allie eased the door shut, and I figured I might as well give it another shot at being the good boarder. "So what's for dinner, wench?"

"Detective Nash, if you know what's good for you, you'll cool the misogynist act and settle down."

"You told me to wait until the door was closed."

"Don't bug me. I need to change. The clothes I'm wearing have been at two crime scenes today and I'm feeling dirty on the outside."

I sunk my tired ass into the sofa. The open bedroom door gave me a clear shot straight across. I figured the woman was letting me know she was dirty on the inside, too. Her familiar body looked pretty good to a man that just this morning left what turned out to be a dead body bleeding out in his bed.

"Are you coming before I run out of hot water?"

I never needed to be asked twice, especially by a beauty like Allie. I forgot all about this morning's body in my own bed.

The sirens wouldn't quit in my nightmare. They wailed and wailed and I thought the bad dream that would never end. The wailing turned into banging on the door. I woke in time for a new nightmare to begin.

"Police! Search warrant! Open up!"

I was in a frigging reality show.

"What the hell is going on?" Allie looked panic-stricken.

Whatever it was, it wouldn't be good for either of us. "I don't know. Answer the door and look. Put something on, just in case it's for real," I warned her.

We scrambled to dress, but we didn't make it. Five cops in riot gear came through the door and swarmed us. I ended up on the floor, thrown there by a cop in full riot gear. Allie ended up beside me, tossed there by the same cop.

A plainclothes cop read us our rights. You're wanted downtown, Nash," he announced.

"By who, exactly?" I needed to know.

"Homicide."

"What the hell? I'm homicide, you dumbasses."

"Shut the fuck up. They're waiting for you downtown. The woman will be coming with you for aiding and abetting." The smug look said it all.

"What the hell is this about?"

"You're wanted for the murder of the firefighter we found in your bed," he announced.

"How was she killed?" I asked.

"You'll hear all about it when you get downtown. Get dressed. And get some clothes on your whore. They want her, too."

The swat team barely left us with time to dress before escorting us out of the building and into separate cruisers for the ride downtown.

I never saw Allie again.

Quite the welcoming committee greeted me at the precinct. The press was on full alert, probably because someone with a hate-on for me let them in on the arrest of a murderer. The sideshow unleashed itself at the underground entrance. From there, all hell broke loose, and I was too consumed with my ordeal to remember to ask about Allie.

No one would have told me, anyway.

I figured they'd try to use her to get to me. It was a classic trick. There was a problem with it, though. I hadn't murdered anyone. Allie wasn't involved in the slightest. If she was smart, she'd lawyer up and be up their asses faster than Velveeta on white bread in a trailer park.

I didn't want a lawyer. I wanted to know what the hell was going on and who was behind it. It was looking like the two murders, the missing woman and the counterfeit operation were all linked. I had no idea how.

It didn't help their case when the two cops asking questions didn't know shit from Shinola. It didn't help that the same interview room I was in was one I used hundreds of times myself. I was pretty comfortable in it, all things considered.

Good cop-bad cop had questions. I was familiar with the play.

"Why did you murder her, Nash?"

Amateurs. Jesus, when I'm done with this, I'm going to have to overhaul the entire homicide department. I don't even think I would have enough time in my life for that shit.

"Murder who? Why did I murder who?"

They exchanged glances. "The woman."

"What woman?" So far, I had two murder cases I was working on. Both involved women.

"The woman found dead in your bed," one insisted.

"You mean Chesterfield? What was the question again?" It never hurt to clarify.

"Why did you murder her?"

"Which her are you talking about?" I still wanted to know. Look guys, we can go around like this all day and all night. I'm an expert at it and it's obvious you're not. So either charge me, place me under arrest and throw away the key, or get me a lawyer.

'We've got proof."

"Sure you do. Show me."

"We don't have to."

They were sounding more and more like little boys rather than paid detectives. "Then charge me and get me a lawyer. Or you both know it's a trumped-up charge and I'm going to walk. Which is it, boyos?"

I had them with that. The gong show slammed the door on their way out. I figured whoever was hiding behind the looking glass went into conference mode. To show me who was boss, it took another four hours before I was kicked and looking for some place to go.

I tried calling Allie, but it went straight to voicemail. I didn't leave a message. I figured that was a clue even I could recognize.

Whoever taped the door to my walk-up made it more than easy to avoid. I ducked and walked into the bloodbath I had been in only yesterday as an observer. The only thing missing was Chesterfield's body. She'd be cooling her slippery heels in the morgue.

I wanted Allie here to help me go through the place. She was that good at crime scenes. There wasn't much she missed. I dug for my phone and started punching in her number, but thought better of it. Eventually, she'd see my call from earlier.

I tossed the place like I was starting my own homicide investigation, and I guess I was. I scoured the joint, looking for anything that might help get me out of the mess my own PD had so eagerly put me in.

It didn't look promising.

The amateurs had done a pretty good job of messing everything up all by themselves. Blood had been tracked from the crime scene into all the rooms. Discarded gloves were scattered on the floor like used condoms. The problem appeared to be that I was the only one seriously screwed over.

If there were any clues left behind, I'd have a hard time finding them without cleaning up the mess left by the clueless. And that's exactly what I did. I cleaned up like I'd been doing it for years.

And I had. Everything, and I mean every single thing, went back to where it was supposed to be. But not before I took photographs and examined every last item like my life depended on it.

Come to think of it, it did.

It was getting on to four a.m. by the time I got everything cataloged. Time to wrap it up for the night. I had a burning desire to march down to the precinct. I wanted to show the professionals how stupid they were.

It wasn't much of a stretch now that I had the shell casing in my hot little hand. The squad missed it. I found it lodged behind a wheel beneath the bed, sunk into the carpet.

No doubt some heads would roll over this, but I didn't call my supervisor. I called an honest lawyer instead. He told me he'd meet up at a coffee shop in the morning. I'd fill him in and we'd proceed to the precinct from there.

Funny how doing all that gave me a new perspective on things. I stretched out on the sofa and didn't come around until ten.

Downtown, it wasn't much of a contest. My honest lawyer smacked them with a cease and desist. When I handed them the bagged empty shell casing, they hemmed and hawed and finally admitted that a mistake had been made. The lawyer was smart enough to ask for a receipt. I never thought of that one. I guess that's why he was a lawyer.

I was happy. But I still had a case to solve.

Whoever framed me had to be a part of the counterfeit ring. Then I remembered the text I ignored while I was busy driving. I hadn't remembered it while I was in the hospital, bouncing up and down on Hank's leg.

I beat a hasty retreat to vehicle impound and dug out my phone from the floor of my side-swiped and wrecked black and white beater. The text came from land title registration at city hall.

I arrived with the same swat team that had assaulted my place. I waited while they set up around the house. The pounding on the door went unanswered. When the ram hit, the door gave way, and every man stormed in.

Nobody. Except a body. It looked to be the second twin. I knew because she had a tattoo on her ass and all of her fingers. I figured it would be no big deal to prove she was Candice Season.

I wanted Allie to get the call-out. Instead, one of her new hires showed up, and I wondered if she sent him on purpose to avoid me. If that was the case, I couldn't blame her. I had pretty much screwed over her career because of the police raid that found me lying low in her apartment.

I let the newbie do his job without introducing myself. I figured he had no need to know whose crime scene it was, anyway. I waited around until I witnessed him taking the victim's prints and a picture of the tramp stamp.

Happy finally, I had somewhere I needed to be.

Candace Season, the victim in the alley, had somehow found her way into the basement of the Fontana Club, possibly by mistake. Possibly her sister, Candice, had turned her onto the place to look for a job. That, or the two were switching out. But why do that?

Candace must have taken a wrong turn and stumbled onto the counterfeiting operation downstairs during a printing run. A nervous printer showed some initiative. He shot her and dumped the body. Then he cleaned up the blood on the floor as best he could and didn't tell anyone about it.

Unfortunately, he didn't notice the counterfeit hundred that found itself dragged upstairs with the girl. It got deposited beneath her when he dumped the body in the alley.

He couldn't have known the woman was Candace Season.

He couldn't have known she had a twin sister, either, so when he took a break and saw Candice Season doing her routine on stage, he figured she was still alive. And that's why Candice went missing. I wondered how stupid the shooter had to be to think he'd witnessed a second coming.

That wasn't the best part, though.

The Fontana Club was owned by old man Season. And he was broke. That's how the heavy-duty printer came on the scene when he advertised space for rent in the basement. It was a perfect cover. So many people came and went to the strip club at all hours that no one would notice.

Until the bodies started piling up.

I still had one problem remaining, though. What the hell was the motive for Chesterfield's murder? And who was the shooter? Someone sure as shit had a hate-on for me.

I took the time to go to Chesterfield's funeral. I figured it was the least I could do, considering she was murdered in my bed. The fire department's brass turned out in their finest. Plenty of cops in blue, too. The damned bagpipes finally got to me. I had to walk away to get some space.

A woman I didn't know stopped me. She looked vaguely familiar, but I didn't recognize her. Then it twigged. Chesterfield had a twin.

"You're Jim Nash."

"You're Chesterfield number two." It wasn't much of a stretch.

"Yes."

"I'm sorry about your sister. She was only trying to make sure I was all right after she pulled my unconscious body from the fire at the Fontana Club."

"I know. She told me she was going to check on you. I told her to keep away."

My reputation had proceeded me yet again. "Maybe we could talk about it sometime—" I didn't think so, but I tried anyway.

"Maybe we could," she said. "Are you in the book?"

"I am."

"Then I'll call you when I'm ready."

I wasn't going to be holding my breath.

I made the long drive back to my empty apartment. I really wanted to talk everything out with Allie. Maybe in the process, we'd come up with something new. She still hadn't called me back. By now, I was smart enough to figure she never would.

The whole trouble with this case was that there were too many loose ends and they were all untied. The most troubling for me was Chesterfield's killing. In my own bed, for Christ's sake. I didn't even know where to start with that one, or if the department would even let me.

For now the best I could do was get some sleep. I stretched out on my sofa and reached to turn out the light. First thing in the morning, I'd go out and get a mattress. Second thing in the morning, I'd be resigning. Content with those decisions, I fell asleep in no time.

I didn't even dream.

SLEEPING WITH A .45

One out of two wasn't so bad.

It was time to spend some money and replace my bed. I picked up the new one to replace Chesterfield's blood-soaked final resting place in what was my bedroom. I cursed at my misfortune for not thinking of having the replacement mattress delivered. I knew I was next to a loser when I was forced to push and pull and drag everything up the flight of stairs, solo. The easiest part was dragging the blood-soaked mattress out the duct-taped, jury-rigged door to the head of the stairway to toss it over the railing to the ground.

Tossing was a misnomer. It was more like huffing and puffing it over the railing and listening as it landed with a satisfying thump on the asphalt below. The bin would be its next destination, but that would have to wait until evening when the temperature dropped to something more manageable.

The letter of resignation was completely forgotten by the effort spent.

My attention span wasn't that short, though. I had a murder to avenge. Bad enough that the murder occurred in my bed. If that wasn't reason enough to keep on keeping on, I didn't know what was.

I didn't want to think about who in the department didn't like me enough to frame me for the killing. That was one reason I stopped thinking about resigning. Instead, I started thinking about a trip to the gun range.

On the way out the door, I picked up a box of fifty and pointed my brand-new black-and-white beater in the gun range's direction. The city refused to assign me a regular unmarked since I'd written off the first. I had to be honest if it came down to it, though. Destruction of city property wasn't entirely my fault. The city wasn't impressed with my honesty.

For the usual reasons, I decided it had to be a crazed former suspect I once crossed paths with who had a hate on. Whoever it was caught up to me while I was going through an intersection. He took it upon himself to seek revenge by parking a semi on top of my brand spanking new unmarked.

Then he disappeared, and I didn't spend any time looking. It was no big deal, and anyway, I lived to tell about it.

While I was in the hospital, the makeshift box in the squad room started filling up with suggestions to get me a time-X'd black-and-white as a poor-man's replacement. Someone higher-up took the hint. The boys in blue lined up three-deep in the break room where the keys were presented.

Never at a loss for words, I produced a stem-winder of an off-the-cuff acceptance speech. By the time I finished, there was no one left to applaud, and I turned the joke around on everybody but me.

My daydream ended with a loud bang and a steering wheel that began an uncommanded turn to the right. So much for happy reminiscing.

The blowout forced the car to climb the curb and jump onto the sidewalk. I picked an alley, pulled in and called for a tow. My mouth watered at the prospect of a forced coffee break at the great little donut shop I frequented across the street from my place.

My mouth didn't water for long. Rather, it went bone-dry. I started to shake and my knees began to rattle. That helped to make it just about impossible to stumble my way back to the car.

Well, all right, it wasn't only that. It was the sound of the gunfire that seemed to be directed toward me. That, and the ducking and dodging I was forced to do did the trick.

The donut would have to wait. So would my trip to the shooting range.

I made it to the car and reached into the dash to retrieve both large-capacity magazines that the city didn't permit me to own. The shakes dispensed with, I found myself in a position to return fire. The unapproved modification to my automatic meant I was able to return fire faster than the rate at which it had been aimed at me.

I dialed in full-auto on the modified handgun. A shadow moved on the rooftop across the street. It was enough to catch my eye. Not sure, I held fire. Another burst of gunfire did it. My police-issue mag emptied in a matter of seconds.

Those damned mags were practically useless when you needed firepower, but it let go with enough hot lead to ensure that the shooter kept his head down. It gave me a chance to insert one of the 33-round mags I pulled out of my car. The satisfying sound it made sliding into the grip almost gave me a hard-on.

Maybe it would have if I wasn't so busy.

I checked the custom lever was still in fun mode before moving along the wall to the foot of the alley. I held there. The shooter's head popped up from the edge of the roof for a look-see. I directed the automatic's muzzle to where it would do the most damage. I got off a spray-and-pray. He wouldn't be expecting an answer-back like that.

I dropped the empty mag and slid home the backup.

The sirens weren't slowing down just yet. I still had a few minutes. I hit the street running and made a jump for the fire escape hanging off the side of the three-story. Huffing and puffing, I hauled my out-of-shape ass to roof-level. I could breathe, barely. A quick recon discovered the only things left behind on the roof were a mess of empty shell casings and a tripod.

I figured my unapproved pistol in full-auto mode must have sent the shooter packing in a hurry. Hell, I'd do the same when I heard that thing barking, whether I knew it was aimed at me or someone else.

My sojourn on the roof left me to discover empty shell casings scattered along the edge of the roof facing the alley. Seven-point-six-two by thirty-nine. Now who the hell was stupid enough to go after a cop with an AK and miss? I picked one up with a pencil and bagged it for future consideration. The rest I left for forensics.

Given that someone in the department attempted to implicate me in the murder of the dead woman discovered in my bed, I was pretty much through trusting anyone with the important things. This morning, one of those important things turned out to be an attempt on my life.

I wasn't sure what I'd do with the shell casing since losing my connection to the forensics lab. Allie, an old flame and one of the city's coroners, had departed for parts unknown after she was arrested, thanks to me. Unfortunately for Allie, she was drawn into my situation when I went to stay with her until the department completed the investigation into the murder victim discovered in my bed.

Allie became caught in the crossfire when the battering ram broke down her apartment door. Thanks to my presence, I got her hauled in for aiding and abetting. That's when she disappeared—not only from my life, but from the city, too.

I wondered if someone convinced her to testify against me, or if she disappeared on her own when she ended up released without being charged. For whatever reason, someone tried to implicate me in a murder, and by association, her as well. I hadn't done the deed, of course, and just because it was my place, didn't stop my fellow officers from doing their jobs investigating.

Now I was back at square one in my personal investigation of the dead woman. Chesterfield. The firefighter. It was personal because the woman was at my place because she was concerned for my well-being after two knocks on the head and a fire.

That she climbed into my bed to keep me warm and wake me up from time to time to check on the progression of my concussion made it personal.

When I left for work that morning, Chesterfield was alive and sleeping. Sometime between then and—

Wait a minute.

Who called in the 911? My apartment was overtop of a partially vacant strip mall. There wasn't anyone around to hear a gunshot.

I headed back to my place. I'd check with the 911 system operators later. In the meantime, I had some basic police work to do. I'd start by canvassing the neighborhood.

I stopped at a gun shop on the way. Flashing my badge waived the mandatory wait for approval. I walked out with a nice, shiny .45 magnum short-barreled revolver and a box of shells to go with it. I had a perfect place to hang it behind my bed in the event someone interrupted my sleeping habits again.

Call me paranoid if you want.

Mindful of my personal sniper, I loaded Mr. Big and Mr. Small, two of the mags for my automatic, from the ammo box I had with me from this morning. I slid Mr. Small home, and I was comfortable again.

I wasn't sure all the door-knocking in the world would come up with anything useful. Citizens didn't want to talk to cops these days. I couldn't blame them. The crazies were always out in force, and when they saw something they didn't like, sometimes they'd do crazy things to people seen talking to the police.

Sometimes, the crazies even drove semis into cop cars.

To hell with the consequences. I had a murder to avenge. That might not be a pretty way for a police detective to put it, but I was beyond caring. The poor woman had been murdered after I left her in the care and comfort of my bed, for crying out loud.

That, and it didn't sit well with me that my space had been invaded—not only by the murderer, but by the cops investigating.

One way or another, I'd get even or die trying.

I ventured out to do some door-knocking. It didn't reveal a lot. Many head-shakings later, I discovered a good-looking dishwater blonde working in the pet shop at the far end of my very own strip mall. I was so unaware of my surroundings I didn't know it was there.

The blonde, I mean. I knew about the pet shop.

I didn't own a dog, but that didn't stop the girl from writing her name on the front of one of the Happy Tail's business cards and handing it across to me. When I was done asking questions, I handed her one of my own. She told me she'd call if she remembered anything.

On my way out the door, I flipped the card and looked at the back. The number there wasn't the same as the one on the front. She must keep a stack by the register, because I never saw her write anything on it except her name. Necessity was still the mother of invention, after all.

When I got back to the precinct, there was a message waiting. It was blondie, and it seems she had a story to tell. I called her back to let her know I'd stop in on my way home after work.

I parked the beater in front of my end of the building and took the sidewalk to the pet shop. By the time I got there, the store was closed. Obviously, a cop wanting to ask questions wasn't a top priority for overtime.

I retraced my steps and discovered a bicycle chained to the foot of my steel staircase. Yes, I'm a cop. No, it wasn't there when I parked. There was a woman at the top of the stairs. She was sitting and waiting patiently like a puppy wanting affection. Her dress was pulled up to let her legs get a bit of sun while she waited. I couldn't wait until she stood up. I wanted to see if the back of her legs were as nice as the front.

In the meantime, I felt a strange urge to bring her a bowl of water and scratch her behind the ears.

"Everyone in the neighborhood knows you're a cop and where you live," blondie volunteered.

Like I needed an explanation, but whatever. I opened the door and invited her in. I knew better, but I wanted to find out what she knew about my stalker and the dead body in my bed. I do have my priorities.

"Want a beer?" I didn't wait for an answer. I popped two Sols and handed her one before she could say no. I figured a little lube would loosen her vocal cords. Besides, I didn't want to drink alone when I had a good-looking girl to share— the drink, not the girl.

Lucy introduced herself with a winning smile and a firm handshake. She took a chair and waited patiently to get started while I hosed down the table. I pulled out my notebook to make it official.

I listened for a bit and then got up to check the fridge for leftovers. Judging by the best-before dates I scrawled on the containers, the Chinese appeared to be good.

"We're going to be a while. We might as well get comfortable." I nuked the glass containers and turned to face her while I waited.

"Don't stop on my account."

"That smells good. Anyhoo, as I was saying—"

Anyhoo? Jesus, who said that any more?

To save the day, the micro's annoying timer sounded. I put plates on the table. Burned my fingers on the glass with the food. Popped the tops off two more Sol. I sat down to share a microwaved dinner with the girl. For good measure, I opened my notebook a second time.

"Take it from the top again," I told her.

She did. She talked non-stop. I'd be lucky if I got to eat.

Lucy just arrived in front of the pet store where she worked. She noticed a van parking in the street outside my end of the vacated strip mall. She fully intended to go over and let whoever it was know that I wasn't home since my car wasn't out front.

She got sidetracked by a Happy Tail customer and unlocked the door to let them into the pet shop instead.

I had no beef with that. Business was business, especially in this neighborhood.

She was about to close the door when she heard two pops. She didn't think anything of it. Most of the cars around here were beaters, just like mine, minus the black and white cop colors. She went into work mode and thought nothing more of it.

"Why didn't you get involved when you found out what went down?" I wanted to know.

"I knew you were a cop. I thought you'd be able to figure out what happened and handle it on your own."

She sounded sincere. "Well, Lucy, just so you know. When I left in the morning, the woman was still warm in my bed, and I mean that in the best way possible. Someone—I don't know who, yet—tried to frame me for her murder. It couldn't have anything to do with jealousy. We only met the day before."

"I don't know any more than I told you. It was a dark-colored van, blue or black. I never thought to look at a license plate," she added.

"Don't worry about it, Luce. You already told me more than I knew before I found you."

"What do you mean?"

"The van," I told her. "It wasn't in any reports. Probably because no one else noticed it."

"In that case, I'm glad I could help." Lucy smiled across the table at me.

I thought I knew the look Lucy was wearing. It was the one that said, Scratch me behind an ear and I'll wag my tail.

"Can I stay here tonight?"

That was plain enough, even for me. I looked her up and down and made sure she noticed me do it. Her legs were long and shaped nicely. Just the right amount of well-toned, tanned thigh peeked out from the hem of her short summer dress. Notwithstanding all that, she had a gorgeous smile.

The sparkling blue eyes convinced me Lucy would be a good house guest. And why not? I already had the .45 stashed behind my brand-new bed.

What could go wrong?

I cooked breakfast for two and managed not to burn anything substantive while a naked Lucy kept me distracted. She seemed to enjoy being close as I moved around the stove. She nuzzled my neck and generally made things take longer than they should.

Only when she got in the way of the frying bacon spatters did she decide she wanted to keep her distance. That only meant she moved off to the side, leaving me with a full frontal. Needless to say—

Eventually, I loaded up the tray and followed her into the bedroom with eyes glued to her finely shaped, slowly swaying backside. Can I help it if I'm a man?

I was trying not to lose my way. Again.

Patiently waiting while she tucked herself in, I balanced the tray. She held aloft the blankets, and I carefully climbed beneath. In half an hour, we shared a cold breakfast under warm, damp sheets. I hoped it showed how considerate I could be by bringing her breakfast in bed—even if it was cold by the time she got to it.

I tried dragging her into the shower, but she wasn't having any of that. Perhaps she could read my mind. She had to be a slave to her job since the owner hardly ever showed up. She chased me out of the bathroom while she prepped for her day.

Apparently, not just anyone could keep my hours.

When the woman stepped out, she was a different person. Somewhere, she came up with a fresh skirt and blouse. A bit of lip gloss and freshly brushed hair that sidelined the bedhead from the night before all worked to impress me. And made me wonder if she was planning for it.

"Good morning, gorgeous. Find your way back after work and we'll scrub down together."

A wide smile adorned her pretty face. "Count on it, Mr. Detective."

"I think we've moved beyond police procedural. Call me Jim," I insisted.

"Very well, Mr. Jim. I'll see you on closing for the grand re-opening." Just to be sure I got it, before she walked out the door, she flashed me, front and back, with a pirouette that forced her dress to mid-thigh, revealing, well, you get the picture. I sure did.

It was my turn to smile.

Luce departed with a satisfied smirk on her face and a gentle sway to her hips. The woman's happy tail bounded down the outside staircase. She stopped to check her bicycle lock. Satisfied, she looked up at me and waved before making her way to work and the Happy Tail pet shop.

I knew I had her. I think she knew the same about me, too, judging by the second pirouette. "I'm going to close early," she called up to me before she disappeared. She wasn't doing any walk of shame, that's for sure.

I made a note to get some laundry done before Lucy returned. Perhaps I might even dust, too. How many times have I said that and never made it? I dressed, got into work mode, and left the door unlocked, just in case.

Yesterday's neighborhood canvass garnered little information of value. Luckily, I discovered Lucy and her description of the dark-colored van. Whether it was involved was another matter. Without a plate, the information wasn't a tremendous help.

A records search would turn up a thousand. There'd be no luck with security cameras, either. None of the few remaining businesses in the neighborhood could afford them.

On my way past the Happy Tail's happy tail, I slowed at the window, honked, and waved in Lucy's direction. She didn't wave back. I turned toward the black van parked on the side street. Its doors were open. That didn't look right. And Lucy did mention that the parked van she saw was dark-colored.

Either someone just dropped off a load of dogs for grooming, or Luce was planning on moving the shop to a new location far from me. I knew right away that wasn't right. We both enjoyed each other's company until she absolutely had to leave for work.

I didn't hear dogs barking when I pulled in behind the van. I got out and went searching for some puppy love. A quick look through the plate glass caught Lucy in the arms of a man. I did a double take, shrugged, and wondered how many men she had on the go.

I would have walked back to my car if it wasn't for catching sight of gun in the man's hand. I reached for my own and slipped the action. From what I could see, there was only one man. Another quick look told me there was something more than a simple robbery going on. The man didn't appear interested in the till.

I eased the door open and let it go against my back. I led with my pistol and carefully entered the store. Lucy saw me and right away I knew it wasn't her first rodeo.

She stomped hard on the man's foot and bent forward at the same time. Her body twisted and she dived for the floor. She slipped from the man's grip and hit the floor hard. I got one off in the man's direction. The explosion in the confines of the store deafened everyone. I didn't hear him hit the floor, but he went down like a slab of meat falling off a hook. The pistol went flying.

He twitched for a bit before I figured it was time to dial 911. He twitched a bit more while I waited for someone to answer. For shits and giggles, I worked a finger into the hole. You know, to stop the bleeding. I wiggled it and the poor bastard couldn't start talking fast enough.

I caught Lucy looking over my shoulder. I didn't see her get up. She slid down and thumped onto the floor. I wasn't worried, though. I hit what I aim for.

When I pulled my finger out of the wound, I had everything I needed. It was just as well. The ambulance arrived and EMTs began scrambling through the door. Thankfully, my interrogation was complete.

"Take a look at the woman on the floor and tell me she's all right," I said to the first EMT through the door.

The EMT didn't miss a beat on his way to the bleeding man on the floor beside Lucy. He took one look, didn't see any blood, and said, She's all right. Cute, too.

A comedian. He was right, though. I took the initiative and rolled Lucy over for a better look. I didn't see any holes. She had her panties on, at least. I knew that without looking since I watched her put them on.

From now on I'd call her lucky Lucy—not that there was any chance in hell I would have hit her. I hit what I aim at.

When Lucy came to, she struggled against me, in a hurry to go into flight mode. I managed to hold her in my arms until she settled down and made up her mind to stay. Good for her. I liked the brave ones—especially when they knew how to handle thieves and dodge bullets. I didn't mind that she wanted to stay in my arms, either, when she snuggled closer.

"I owe you another dinner for that performance, and I'm not talking about the one you gave last night." I caught a glance from the EMT. He shook his head and went back to work.

Lucy formed a weak smile. "For the rest of my life, you can have anything you want."

I was high-fived by both EMTs as they wheeled out the cradle. On the way by, I snapped a pic of the guilty party's face for good measure. I had a lot of mug shots to search through.

"Hey Luce. When you're finished tonight, can I pick you up?"

I was pleased as punch when she nodded in a hurry and said yes. I was even happier when she asked if she could keep her bike chained to my staircase while she waited.

I hoped she wouldn't think I was too eager. I heard somewhere it was good form to wait a few days before asking for a second date. Then I began thinking that perhaps Lucy wouldn't have imagined last night to be a date.

"I left my door unlocked for you," I let her know.

Little did she know that the yes she gave me would force her to eat fast food while she spent the night at the precinct.

Was this a blossoming romance or what?

I had my social life locked up. I headed for the van by the side of the building. I pulled on the rubber gloves and began with the driver's side. There wasn't anything too exciting there. I opened the opposite door and empty beer cans rattled to the ground.

So maybe he was on a stakeout.

There was something about the green and yellow bandana hanging from the driver's mirror that piqued my curiosity. Nothing jumped out at me, though. I tucked it into my pocket along with the rental receipt. It corresponded with the sticker I spied on the rear bumper when I did my walk-around.

The good stuff turned up when I moved into the back of the van. I found a spent cartridge. A pool of dried blood on the floor had to have been whispering my name, too. There was some spatter on the side and the roof. I made the call and waited for someone to show up who would know more than I did.

In the meantime, I went to check on Lucy. There wasn't a sign of the struggle remaining. The blood was wiped and everything straightened up. I found her in a back room, bathing a dog in a mess of shampoo.

She looked up and grinned when she saw me. "You sure know how to treat a girl."

"I thought you'd appreciate it. That's why I asked you out right away for tonight. I wanted the shock factor. It worked out when you didn't hesitate."

She smiled up at me again, and I knew I was home. "Is it going to be a regular date, or will I need body armor?"

"I think we'll be safe. In fact, I can almost guarantee it," I assured her.

"Almost guarantee? Good to know." She kissed me on the cheek. It was a tossup which of us beamed the brightest. "Now get out of here." She gently eased me toward the door. "I have a dog to bathe."

The dog looked like a Black Labrador beneath all the foam. He looked at me like he knew what I was up to before he barked a warning. I think it said Don't mess with my woman or you'll be sorry.

The coroner's vehicle arrived as I walked out the door. I waited while they sampled the blood in the back of the van. I called for a tow to haul the van to impound and high-tailed it to the rental company. No one behind the counter recognized the photo of the results of my target practice. The renter's ID turned out to be fake.

Back to square one.

The text from the department's vehicle shop informed me that yesterday's blowout in front of my favorite donut shop wasn't the result of a bad tire. It was a gunshot. I didn't figure on that. Someone knew I'd be going past and took advantage. What I couldn't figure is how they knew.

Then I realized it was whoever had the place staked out. The coffee shop was one of my favorite places to take a break. I liked it because the little hole-in-the-wall was one of my hideouts for a quiet cup of coffee and innocent flirting with Mabel, the owner. I never told anyone about it.

It was time to get up on the roof across the street for a better look. And sure enough.

The sleeping bag behind the chimney was the first clue. The second was the pile of cans and the gas burner. Christ, they were patient, to say the least. That spelled grudge to me. I missed it earlier because it was on the long end of the strip mall, almost directly overtop of my place.

I ran through a list of who in my world hated me enough to set out to kill me. Being a cop, the list wasn't short, but even so. To go to this much trouble meant some serious problems on the part of the shooter. Nobody I knew had the patience for this.

At least, I didn't think I knew anyone.

Hell, even in my wildest imagination I couldn't think of anyone wanting to be rid of me this badly.

Not even the ex-girlfriends, and that was saying something.

Not even Allie.

With no leads beyond fingerprints on the empty cans, I packed a couple away in a plastic bag and headed for the precinct. To kill time, I took a seat in front of my monitor and scrolled through mug shots. Nothing jumped out at me. I turned off the monitor.

I hoped the extra set of eyes I'd bring to the game tonight would do the trick. At least, with Luce it wouldn't be as boring. I hated to admit it, but I was starting to like the girl.

As far as the actual case went, I still had little to go on.

What I had was a dead body. As far as I knew, there was no motive for the body to be in my bed, other than that Chesterfield invited herself into it while she was alive. I had a roof shooter who camped out for God only knows how long to get his crack at me. Fortunately, he missed. And I didn't know what I did to piss him off, either.

The campsite on the roof was another thing. The way the shooter had that positioned gave him an opportunity to listen in on what went on in my apartment. I wondered if he knew I had a woman in bed with me, and for some sick reason decided to make it personal.

I should probably go back to Chesterfield's place to look for boyfriend photos. I didn't. Something else was bugging me.

The neckerchief I found hanging in the van was waving like a red flag, even though it was green. It was only a damned bandana. Nothing special there. Even Lucy used one as a sweat band when she rode her bike. I know because every once in a while, before I knew who she was, I used to check her out when she rode on by.

I remember thinking she was kind of young. And I sure as hell didn't realize that she worked at the pet shop.

That was then. Now I knew Lucy was just right.

I picked up some Chinese and headed back to the pet shop. She left her bike tied up and my place and we drove to the precinct. I let her have the chair at the keyboard before producing the takeout.

"You really go all out when you ask someone on a date, don't you?"

I showed my teeth in a toothy grin and she grinned back. "I don't want to spoil you right off," I said. "I want to work up to it."

"In that case, you must have brought me here for a reason. Either that, or you're testing me."

"Maybe a little of both. I need your help," I said.

"You'll have to feed me first."

That was easy, so I did.

We exchanged dog stories and cop stories and before we knew it, it was midnight. We were laughing almost the entire time. It seemed as though we both enjoyed each other's company.

Maybe even a little too much.

Lucy was a small-town girl who grew up on a farm. She was even a former 4-H girl. She moved to the city for adventure and education, where she was taking a year off before her final year and graduation. The pet shop was the perfect job where she could still work with animals, yet be free to finish her education when she was ready.

"I still wear the 4-H bandana."

So that's what I saw her wearing on her bicycle.

"I don't like to brag, but I'm a former Cub scout." Already I was feeling a certain kinship with the woman.

"You didn't finish the program, did you?"

Was I that transparent? "Not really," I admitted.

"Why not?"

"That's a story all by itself," I said.

"Well, since we'll be here all night, and I'm going to be busy trolling the mug shots, you can entertain me."

I got Lucy set up and comfortable with snack food and water, and she was good to go. When I could see she was settled in and familiar with the software, I set her free.

"You're going to get the condensed version, because—"

"You listened to me ramble on about my boring life in a small town. Now it's your turn to bore me about growing up in the bright lights and big city."

"Well, not exactly. Truth be told, I grew up in a small town, too. Not as small as yours, though. It was a factory town. One industry. A lunch-bucket town. Shift work. The plant ran twenty-four and seven."

I stopped to remember how all of us in the same crowd got the hell out as fast as we could after high school. We couldn't put the place in the rear-view fast enough.

"Keep going. I can type, use a mouse, look and listen, all at the same time. It's called multi-tasking for you old timers."

"Ouch. Sorry. I got lost." I smiled, and she smiled, and I was smitten. "Anyway, in grade three or somewhere near to it, I belonged to Cubs. One of the guys I met there, Gordie, eventually became a pretty good friend. He lived out in the country and rode the bus to school. When he could, he hung out at my place and we'd do the usual kid stuff in town."

"Now you're just a city slicker trying to kiss up to a country girl, aren't you?"

"I swear on a stack of 4-H posters," I grinned at her. "One day, Gordie shows up at my place and starts telling me about his older brother. Ron. Gordie told me Ron picked on him all the time. He said when he got really mean he'd load the .22 in front of him and threaten him with it.

"These days they call that bullying."

"I know that. I'm talking a generation ago, at the very least."

"Just how old are you?" Lucy asked.

"If you're patient, maybe I'll let you count the rings later tonight."

She looked around the deserted floor, lit dimly by blue computer screens. "If you don't keep talking, I just might take you up on it right now."

It was an offer I could hardly refuse but for the location. "Well, Gordie didn't show up at school for a couple of days. Then, out of the blue, the principal announces that Gordie wouldn't be coming back to school. The poor kid committed suicide."

"Oh dear. I'm sorry, Jim."

"Yeah, well, all the Cubs were at Gordie's funeral. His folks wanted him buried in his uniform, so we got to do the honor guard thing and all."

I had forgotten how long ago it happened.

"The funny thing is, after it was all over with, Gordie's brother, Ron, somehow showed up at the playground one day. I'm not sure if he was looking for me. Maybe he was just passing by. But, when I saw him, I could tell by the way he looked at me. Gordie must have told him I knew what was going on.

"Are you sure? That was a long time ago."

"I'm as sure as I can be. Ron gave me a look that went from almost saying hello to abject fear in about a split second. I never saw or heard anything about him after that."

Lucy interrupted my storytelling. "Here's the mug shot you're looking for, Nash."

"Are you sure?"

"As sure as I can be."

It had to be the Ouch-oww-dammit! cries that woke me up. Like the good cop I am, I immediately set out to investigate. I crossed paths with a naked woman. She was standing in front of the stove, trying to dodge spatters coming off of the bacon frying in the pan.

I had to admit, she had some damned fine hip action going on. "You've never done that before, have you?"

"What do you think?"

I took off my robe and wrapped her up, but not before copping a feel. Top and bottom. "I'll be in bed when you get finished with that."

"By the time I'm finished with you, you'll be wanting to stay there to rest up."

"Promises," I said, and grinned my way back to the bedroom and the still-warm bed.

A faint sound of stones crunching underfoot filtered through the ceiling. I'm not known as the best housekeeper, but even I managed to keep rocks out of my palace.

"Lucy! Turn it off and get in the bedroom right now."

"But I'm not finished yet," she insisted. "I wanted to surprise you."

"You did. You can finish your surprise later. There's someone on the roof."

I got out of bed and pulled Lucy into the bedroom. I pushed her down on the floor beside the mattress. I threw clothes in her direction and tried to keep calm. It didn't work until I got my pants on.

Just soon enough.

The front door crashed onto the floor. Heavy footsteps calmly marched in and stomped through my living room. Lucy started to get up. I couldn't let her do that. I knocked her down and reached for the brand-new .45 stashed at the head of the bed.

"Stay down this time. And don't come out of here until I tell you it's all clear. Understand?"

She didn't answer. Damn. I must have knocked her out when I pushed her down the second time. I pulled back the hammer and slowly made my way into the kitchen, trying not to give up my position.

Nobody.

I led with the .45 and edged around a wall into the living room.

Nothing.

I looked in the closet. Nothing there, either. I eased the hammer down and tucked the .45 into my pants and called to Lucy. "It's clear. You can come out now."

I propped the door up in its frame and tried making it look halfway secure. I couldn't, and it wasn't. Blue sky showed through the edges where it was torn off its hinges and separated from the frame.

I went searching for Lucy. I found her in the bedroom. She was sitting on the edge of the bed, naked, holding her head in her hands. I eased her down, lifted her feet, and covered her with the sheet. I grabbed a bag of frozen peas out of the freezer, retrieved what was left of breakfast, and made a production of presenting it. "I'll have flowers for your breakfast tomorrow, Luce."

She wasn't having any of it. She skipped breakfast and instead held the ice-cold bag against her swollen eye. "The way things are going around here we might not have a tomorrow."

I didn't want to contemplate that. "We'll have plenty of tomorrows. I know it, and so do you." I slipped under the sheets and snuggled up. She stopped shaking eventually.

Lucy was sleeping on her stomach when I slipped the covers off. With her firm, untanned rear staring me in the face, I couldn't resist giving it a little squeeze. I followed up with a firm slap.

"Ouch. You bastard. Stop that."

"That's not what you said last night."

To kiss up, I squeezed the other cheek. Damn but that was one firm bit of woman. Distracted as I was, I traipsed to the kitchen and rummaged through her backpack. I came up with a wallet. I never really thought age was a problem, but now I knew for sure.

I blinked twice and opened the wallet again to check before putting it back. Triplets?

"What are you doing out there?" Lucy called.

"I'm making breakfast."

"I don't have time. I have to get to the shop."

"I'll bring it to you. A woman shouldn't go to work on an empty stomach."

"Such a sweet man," she said. "How come no one's got you in their pocket?"

"Well, so far, you seem to be the one to have filled your pocket with me."

"I'm leaving my stuff here. Is that all right?"

"Of course it is— Oh, you're wearing another dress."

Luce twirled. Her skirt billowed and settled against tanned legs. I couldn't stop grinning, and the subtle smile on her face convinced me she liked me, too.

"Yes, I like. Now stop teasing and get going. I'll see you in a couple with breakfast."

"You're spoiling me."

"Yes I am. Will I regret it when you get home?" Home? That slipped out, somehow, but then I was always saying things like that to the women I liked. I couldn't help myself.

"Most likely not." She twirled again, lifted the door out of the frame and leaned it against the wall. "I won't need a key."

Lucy clip-clopped down the steps until I couldn't hear her. I started thinking I might be falling in like when an explosion echoed off the buildings across the street.

Lucy.

I raced to pull on pants and a shirt and reached for the .45 tucked into the headboard. I jumped down the stairs in panic mode. She was on the street on the way to work. It couldn't be her shop. My mind went full speed to comprehend what had happened. What was happening.

It was an echo. It had to be. It wasn't so strong of an explosion. I hit the street running and rounded the corner of the building. No broken windows across the street. No crashed vehicles on fire. Maybe it was only a door come out of a frame to crash onto the ground. Still, it couldn't be good.

The cloud of dust, black smoke and destruction hit me like a brick. The sudden realization that Lucy must have just that instant put her key in the lock and pushed open the door would have brought me to my knees were I not running so fast to get to her.

I wanted to keep on going. I wanted to run past and keep running. I knew if I did, I wouldn't stop. I couldn't. My legs would keep putting one foot in front of the other. I didn't have a guess where or when I might stop.

I found her on the ground, off to the side of the door. She was behind the cement block wall, protected from the main force of the blast. I dropped to the ground beside her. Reached for her writs. Her pulse was strong and racing. Her breathing shallow. Her face and arms were covered in small cuts and scrapes consistent with shattering glass. From what I could see, blood loss appeared minimal.

Her dress was in tatters. I put my coat over her and took her in my arms.

"You're going to be all right, Luce," I tried to reassure her.

"Easy for you to say, you bastard. You're not the one wearing the shredded summer dress that I pulled out of my backpack just for you."

"If it's any consolation, it still looks pretty good on you." That was no lie.

"You're only saying that because you can see right through it."

"Well, now that you mention it—" I countered.

The ambulance screeched to a stop beside us, and I left Lucy to the professionals. The EMT recognized me and shook his head. Lucy had a last wish for me.

"Jim. See if there's a dog in there. She came in last night. Her name is Zelda."

"I'll be over to see you in a bit. And yes, I'll take good care of Zelda. I promise."

The fire trucks parked farther away and men scrambled to lay hose and take up positions. There wasn't much fire left for them. It was almost as if the blast was meant to cause minimal damage by blowing out the store windows and nothing else.

I rushed into the back of the building and discovered freshly bathed Zelda from yesterday. I unlocked her cage, found a leash, and let her limp into the picture for Lucy just before the door slammed on the ambulance. Not sure what to do once she lost sight of Lucy behind the closed ambulance door, Zelda sat down beside me. I scratched her behind the ear. Her wet nose found my hand and she snuffled.

Still unsure, the huge black Labrador looked up at me with sad brown eyes and a hangdog expression.

"Yes, Zelda. That's pretty much how I feel about the situation, too."

She woofed and got up and followed me home. We both slowly made our way up the stairs. She lapped up the water I put out. When she finished, I took her on a tour of the place. She sniffed and snuffled her way into the bedroom.

Zelda looked up at me once, jumped up onto the bed, and settled in to stretch out on my side of it.

Women.

I smiled and thanked my lucky stars—for women, not the dog. Okay, well, maybe just a little for the dog, too. She seemed to be a bit of a sweetheart.

Zelda appeared to be settling in nicely. She was on my bed, wheezing, dreaming of green fields filled with flowers, tennis balls, and shallow ponds. At least, that's what I'd be dreaming about if I was in her place. I headed off for dog food and duct tape.

I used all the tape to give the door a jaunty tilt. With a bit of help it closed from both inside and out. I'd worry about locking it later.

For my own safety I needed to find out what the hell was going on. It wouldn't hurt if Lucy and Zelda could learn to relax around me, too. I drove into the seedy part of town and checked into a couple of bars that I thought might turn up the shady characters I needed.

I came up empty. Then I hit the Blue Parrot.

Jerry, the Parrot's bartender, was a former customer. He ended up on the wrong end of a heist gone bad and did five with time off for good behavior, thanks to me. He put his time inside to good use and learned woodworking. When he got out he approached me for a loan.

I was dubious at first. What cop wouldn't be given the human disasters they dealt with on a daily basis?

The first thing I did was check his prison record. It was a good one. He kept his nose clean for the entire time spent behind bars. His wife and family stood by him. He showed me a rough business plan. He'd worked it up on the back of a couple of big brown envelopes.

I took a chance and loaned Jerry some of the cash after he convinced me he could make a go of it. He set up shop in a rental unit and did custom woodworking for kitchen rebuilds. When business was slow, he tended bar to take up the slack.

He owed me, even though he'd paid the bill a long time ago. He knew it, too.

I offered Jerry the opportunity to fix my door. He accepted on the spot. I filled him in on what was going on. I told him about the shooting attempt on my life by the sniper. The break-in at my place could have been anyone. The explosion at the pet shop that injured Lucy was pretty bold. He agreed with that.

In about a second he nodded his head toward two men hunched over a table in a dark corner. They were deep in conversation, oblivious to anything else in the bar. It was time to take care of business.

The new guys in the precinct liked those spring-loaded extending saps. I never wanted to waste time pulling it out and waiting for it to expand. While it could administer a good rap, it took too long to swing.

My preference was for the old leather and shot variety. I wore it in a pocket fitted on the left side of my pants. Short and flexible, in close quarters it made it easy to flip out and break a collarbone or badly bruise a forearm at the drop of a glass.

That's what I did when the moron jumped out of his chair and waved a fist in my direction. The fist changed into an open hand as he went down on his knees clutching a badly bruised collarbone. For good measure, I let him have a quickie on the side of the head. There was no complaining when he went all the way down.

It was over so quick, the second bozo decided he had to put up or shut up. He jumped up into a fighting stance and I knew right away he wasn't going to be a patsy. I didn't mess around. When he saw the automatic leveled at his chest he straightened up the chair he was in and sat his ass back down.

"I've got a witness that puts you pretty close to where someone was killed," I let him know.

"Tough luck for her, then."

I smacked him on the collar with the butt of my gun and he fell out of the chair and went down like a cow walking into a slaughterhouse. I called for the wagon and stood guard at the bar with Jerry, drinking Canada Dry.

"You better hope they keep those two. They look to me like the type that hold a grudge."

"That's the trouble, Jerry. They've been holding a grudge for too long."

I went by the station to clear up the mess of paperwork I had on account of the two in the bar. I finished and it was time to pick up Lucy. I went by home and picked up Zelda. She was happy to see me and did her business the minute she was downstairs.

"Good girl, Zelda." I fished a treat out of a pocket and handed it over. Not satisfied, she was busy sniffing my hand for another. "We don't have time for more treats," I said.

She didn't believe me. She sat down and it looked like she wasn't about moving.

"We're going to pick up Lucy. Do you want to come?" That got her moving in the right direction. I opened the back door and she barked. It sounded like shotgun to me, so I let her in the front. Right off she sat down on the seat and began looking intently out the front window trying to hurry me up.

I stopped for flowers on the way. The old girl behind the desk gave me a tip about a dress shop across the street and already I figured I was one up on Lucy's last beau.

The gift wrapping took a couple of minutes. Petting and scratching Zelda took a couple more, and I was on my way. Lights flashing in the grill managed to move some of the cars out of the way and next I knew I was parked beside a fire hydrant like it was reserved parking just for me.

I checked in with hospital registration. No one could see Zelda below the counter. We ended up in a waiting room. Lucy appeared in a hospital gown, limping but otherwise unharmed. She and Zelda would be a couple for a bit, sharing limps and my bed.

"How long have you been here?" Zelda looked she wanted to tell her, but she couldn't talk. The dog walked circles around Lucy, worrying with every step.

Lucy didn't look so bad. A bit pale, perhaps. I would be, too.

"An hour or so. I wasn't going to leave until we got to see you. What happened to your clothes?"

"A nurse threw them out," she said.

"In that case, you better put that gown on the opposite way. Every man in this place is going to be asking for your phone number when they get a gander at your fine rear end walking itself out of this pop stand.

"I'll give them yours. Are those for me?" she wanted to know.

I grinned like a teenager caught out before he was ready to hand over the flowers. Lucy's grin wouldn't allow her to close her lips when she kissed my cheek.

Zelda snuffled and worried and got ear scratches from both of us. Her tail never halted its floor sweeping.

I debated about letting Lucy have her presents so soon. I figured if I wanted to be on her good side—which right about now in that gown was her backside—I'd better let her have the dress. She wasted no time ripping open the box, smiling the whole time.

"Did you get underwear?" she wanted to know.

Damn. I never thought about that. Then I remembered. "You stopped wearing underwear when you started seeing me. Don't you remember?"

Luce gave me a devilish look. "Right. How could I forget?"

I patted her rear. Lucy skipped a couple of steps. Zelda wheezed and snuffled. An old girl at reception smiled in our direction. It all made me very happy.

"I rounded up the man you identified in the mug shot. For good measure I added the guy he was with."

I opened the car door and Lucy eased her way down into the seat. Zelda settled for the back seat.

"I'm sore all over. I can't wait to get home."

"You took quite a beating," I had to admit.

"I'll manage with a bit of help."

"Zelda waited faithfully. You should have seen her performance until she picked up your scent and headed straight for the bedroom and my side of the bed.

"Does she remind you of anyone in particular?"

The last time I checked, Lucy was fast asleep where she belonged, on my side of the bed. The black Lab, Zelda, was relegated to having her doggie dreams while sprawled on the floor beside her.

The dress hung on the door frame, waiting for her to wake up. If I was a lucky man, and I thought I was, I'd get to help her into it before too long.

I'd be even luckier when I got to help her out of it for the second time.

* * *

Pounding. Pounding. What? No. It couldn't be. My brain asleep couldn't fathom it. Groggy and half-awake, I swung feet to floor, stood up, unsteady, and stumbled to the kitchen. Lucy's hands were around the grip on the .45 that belonged behind my bed.

"What the hell—"

The scent of gunpowder tainted my nostrils. The pounding had been gunshots, thanks to Lucy and no thanks to my rudely interrupted dream.

"How many did you get off?" I asked.

"Two."

"You hold that thing like a pro."

"My dad taught us."

"Good to know."

She cast her gaze to the ceiling. "There's a hole in the roof. I hope it doesn't rain."

I followed her eyes. "Yeah, those .45s pack a pretty good recoil."

"I'll do better next time now that I know how to hold it down."

"So—"

"So I thought I heard someone trying to get past our duct-tape door. I couldn't wake you up. I figured it was my responsibility to take matters into my own hands."

"Has anyone told you lately you look like a barrio girl?"

"It's the missing eyebrows, isn't it?"

I grinned at her. "Yeah, but that can be fixed with a little eyeliner."

"How long have you been checking out the chulas in the barrio?" she wanted to know.

"Long enough."

Lucy held out the .45 butt-first. I slipped the cylinder and reloaded. "For next time."

I tucked the .45 back into the hiding spot behind the bed before calling the precinct. I inquired about the two from the bar I bruised and hauled in earlier. I waited on hold until someone came back and said they were still in lockup.

All right, so there had to be something else going on. Whatever it was, I was in the dark. I figured I'd better get a clue pretty fast before I ended up getting Lucy killed for my ignorance.

Raindrops began hitting the windows. I moved Zelda's water dish to where I thought it might collect some of it from the hole in the roof. With the dog looked after, I gave my full attention to Lucy. "I'm kind of getting accustomed to seeing you naked around these parts."

"By the look of it, I'd say you're not so accustomed to it just yet."

Which, as it turned out, was a pretty good thing as far as we were concerned. Zelda, too.

My tired body reluctantly crawled its way out of a bed warmed by the two women in my life. Okay, so one of them was four-legged. Snicker if you want, but the other one was no dog, I can guarantee that—even if she was still a little worse for wear and missing just a bit of her eyebrows.

My pub crawl began early and started with every bar I could remember that opened at six a.m. The rewards weren't great. One was the odor of stale beer and cigarettes, with the occasional bit of puke thrown in for free. Sleepy, disinterested bartenders revealed nothing.

When I finished with that run of mildly unhappy bartenders, it was time to move on to the ten a.m. crowd. Ditto on the results.

No big surprise.

If I learned anything so early in the morning, it was being in the bar industry meant profit, if there was indeed any, never ended up being reinvested in the business. Rather, it seemed to go into shiny vehicles, drugs, and the occasional good-looking waitress, not necessarily in that order.

Bullshit seemed to play a big part in it, too.

By high noon it began to look like my legwork would be wasted. Then I hit the Blue Parrot again, and wouldn't you know it, jackpot. And I didn't even play the lottery.

Maybe I'd start.

The only two customers in the place must have thought I was blind. They edged out, and I edged out behind them, hot on the trail. My reward was a knock on the head. The last thing I remembered seeing was dirty asphalt and stars— and we're not talking about the walk of fame here.

I came to in the back of a step van. It was parked across the street from my apartment. The barking dog clued me in that something was going on that I wouldn't like. Even if I couldn't, at least Zelda was doing a job trying to take care of Luce.

I knew Lucy had done her job when the .45 she must have hauled out from behind my bed did its job. I wondered how many holes there'd be in the roof after this episode. I shouldn't have worried. When the door opened and Lucy was thrown in with me, I knew I wouldn't have to worry about holes manufactured by the .45.

"You're definitely attracting the wrong crowd with that chula makeup you're wearing." I wanted to keep it light.

"Thanks to you again. I think I better find another guy while I still can."

"Oh come on. What's not to like about a man and his faithful companion?"

"Might I remind you it was me who came up with Zelda?"

"You could, but it won't do you any good now."

We were in deep shit, and we knew it. We knew it was entirely my fault, too. The only positive thing to come out of it was that they had used my own handcuffs on me.

I had the solution for that.

The criminal element driving the van obviously hadn't seen any cop shows on TV. They completely missed the backup in the holster strapped to my ankle. I snuggled up to Lucy and got the cold shoulder.

"If you think that's going to help your cause, you're sadly misinformed," she warned me.

"You say that now, but let me whisper in your ear for a minute."

When I was done she maneuvered into position to wiggle fingers into my pocket. She reached bottom and came up empty-handed.

"Maybe it's the other one."

I struggled like a porpoise in an aquarium out of water. I huffed and puffed myself into a position where I figured Lucy could search the opposite pocket. Despite her encouragement for me to lose a few pounds of muffin top, I had difficulty positioning myself for her to reach the key.

The van bumped and groaned down alleys and across back streets. By the time it stopped we were in no better shape. We'd been subjected to more bumps and bruises than a bad pole dancer and we still hadn't found the handcuff key or a way out.

With both sets of hands behind us, reaching the gun on my ankle wasn't an option.

Brakes squealed and both front doors slammed. We were alone again. We readjusted and this time Lucy dragged the key out of me. In no time she had one side undone and I slipped my wrist free, twisted away from her and slipped off the other cuff.

First things first. I freed my backup and had to set it down to struggle with the duct tape wrapped around Lucy's ankles. I moved to her wrists. She recognized one of her captors walking past the front of the van. Her eyes locked on and her free hand snaked to the gun on the floor.

In the van's confined cargo deck the explosion was deafening.

"Did you get him?" I yelled.

"I think so."

I took my chance and did a quick look out the back. There wasn't a thing around but a couple of cars parked close to one lonely storage shed made from a series of linked cargo containers. They sat on a cement pad, at just the right height for the van.

"Do you think you can back this thing up against that door?" I asked.

"You know it. Say when."

Lucy squeezed through the narrow door into the cab. I lifted the rear door all the way up. I had a clear view behind us. She backed the van until it bumped against the loading dock.

The overhead door wound up and two men began throwing bundles into the back of the van. Faithful employee that I was, I helped stack them in the truck.

There was half a load by the time we finished. I slapped the divider and Lucy shifted into drive and we were off. Where the hell we were going was anyone's guess if you didn't know I was a cop. "Take us to the precinct, Luce. I'll ride shotgun."

I climbed into the front, adjusted the mirror, and settled in. I knew it wouldn't be long before someone started wondering who it was driving off with the missing cargo.

"What I wouldn't give for a pay phone right about now."

"Good luck with that," she said.

A couple of things bothered me. I didn't have a clue what was going on. Yes, we had extricated ourselves from handcuffs and duct tape. Yes, I had a truckload of dope and I was headed toward the nearest cop shop. Yes, we had a meth lab and a body that needed to be called in.

So then, why were we taken in the first place? "I know I'm in the clear on this, and I don't like to cast any stones, but is there something you're not telling me I should know?"

"Well—"

"Spill, woman."

"The murdered woman in your bed, the firefighter, was my sister," she volunteered.

So that was it. "I feel guilty as hell about that. I can't figure who killed her, or why. And by the way, I checked your ID and discovered you had the same last name. Until then, I only figured as much. You look nothing like her."

"Our parents lost our home in all the financial shenanigans that went on. My dad had to find another line of work, so he went on a road trip to Mexico and carted home a load of coke."

"Okay, I'm covering my ears now." I mimed it.

"He made enough to pick up a distress sale and we ended up with a smaller home at a good price. The roof didn't leak and there was just enough space for the five of us."

I could see where she was going with this already. The locals took offense with having their business profits cut, and wanted to leave a message. The one they left dead in my bed was it.

With Lucy working just down the street, it wouldn't be long before the message got out.

Now I was stuck with a drug-dealing family, and two of their offspring had ended up in my bed. I figured I was doing good, though. Only one of them was dead.

So far.

At least now I knew drugs played a part in the shit I had going on in my life. It never ceased to amaze me how drugs could screw up even a simple piss-up in a brewery. I wasn't even a serious drinker.

"There's a truck behind us. Do you think it's trouble?"

"There's no doubt. Someone finally figured out the drugs have left the building, and not with who they thought."

It all happened too fast. The dually truck swerved and pulled out to pass. Lucy's attempt at pushing harder on the pedal went to nothing on the underpowered step van. The driver of the dually came up beside Luce. He cranked the wheel. The vehicles made contact. The unstable, top-heavy step van careened off the pavement.

Lucy swerved and over-corrected in a vain attempt to keep the heavy van on the pavement. The front tire left the road and dug into the loose windrow of sand on he side. She cranked the steering wheel around, overreacted and over-corrected again, and the van flipped onto its side. It continued on its way, careening into a ravine, finally slowing to a stop.

When the dust settled, the driver's door was gone. I couldn't see Lucy. She had disappeared. Either she skipped out or she wasn't wearing her seatbelt. I climbed out and almost fell on top of her limp body. I checked for a pulse.

Lucy was gone.

Ditto for the dually.

I quick-marched my bruised ribs down the road, eventually ending up at a house. I called in a SWAT team to raid the meth lab if the fools hadn't moved out already. Perhaps they'd think it all blew over when the van disappeared. That, or they were too stoned on fumes to realize their operation had been compromised.

I allowed Lucy to rest in peace. I did my duty as a cop and a man and explained the situation as best I could to her folks. To myself I pleaded ignorance and let them think I knew nothing.

I stayed away from the funeral.

How could I do anything else? I was responsible for the deaths of two. They still had one sister left, but I was going to stay far away from her for as long as I could.

To me, that meant forever.

Even if it was her turn for some comforting.

I'm not a television cop. Those guys solve their cases in an hour. Less than that if you included all the sales pitches for beer and groceries. Forty minutes plus a couple—that's all it took.

For me, it worked out to a lifetime.

If it feels like it's time to go, it usually is. The day before, I handed in my badge, my gun, my cell phone and the keys to the black and white beater.

I was gone.

She must have known I was packing. She came and looked into the bedroom a couple of times. Every time she would stop at the door, turn around and walk away. It was as if she didn't believe it, or wouldn't believe it, or wasn't sure.

Eventually, she got tired of waiting and stopped coming in. By then I was finished packing. I hauled my bag and Lucy's backpack down the steps to a waiting Zelda. She sniffed the bag and wagged her tail.

There was no way I could tell her that Luce wouldn't be coming with us. I threw her bag into the trunk and opened the door for the dog. She happily jumped in and sat up front. Zelda's tail wagged like there was no tomorrow. Which was true, for some of us.

Zelda's cold nose found my neck and I laughed and she did it again because she could.

I wasn't so happy, though. I wondered if I ever would be again. I don't think Zelda was very happy, either.

PIRATE CAY

1

I finished packing and went looking for Zelda. Usually, when I was done filling a suitcase, she'd be in the kitchen, sulking by her food bowl, knowing she was off to the kennels for a short stay. She must have figured something different was up, because this time, I found her sulking by the door.

I don't know how, but Zelda knew we were going off somewhere together. The instant she saw me, her ears perked up and her tail started to thump the floor, making noise like an upstairs neighbor on a dance-a-thon. Smart dog that she was, she read the clues and knew there would be no kennel in her life this time.

To keep her happy on our road trip, I grabbed the bag of food from under the counter, and her food dish. For good measure, I added the water bowl. With food and dishes in one hand and my bag in the other, we walked down the stairs to the car.

I popped the trunk and stowed everything I could. Zelda, ever the nervous Nellie, stayed far enough away to make sure I didn't make an attempt to put her in there, too. I closed shop, and she woofed agreement before scurrying to the driver-side door, satisfied I had everything she needed.

Zelda never actually called shotgun, but I knew she liked to ride up front. I opened the door, and she jumped in and squatted on the front passenger seat like she belonged. Which she did. There was no question. We both knew it.

I got in and slammed my door and Zelda barked once like she was the boss. Like she wanted me to hurry up and get on with it.

Women.

For a change, I checked texts on my phone and discovered more than a couple from Allie. We had a fling about a year-and-a-half ago. When the fling ended, we stayed on good terms—don't ask me how—and every once in a while we ended up consoling one another for whatever reason.

Well, okay, so we stayed on good terms until she got caught up in one of my murder cases. It was probably my fault more than hers for letting that happen. Following her arrest and release without charges, she blew town for parts unknown. Somehow, I knew I'd never hear from her again.

Thus my surprise at the stack of waiting texts. Maybe I should turn on my phone more often—especially if it meant I'd get to pick up Allie's messages. Strike that never-hear-from-her-again discussion.

I brought up the number pad, figuring I should call to find out what was going on. My phone died at that moment and that idea went out the window. I couldn't find a charge cord within easy reach. Zelda was no help. I'd have to stop later to water and exercise Zelda. I'd find the spare cord in my bag when I did.

Originally, I planned on heading down the Keys with Zelda on a well-deserved vacation. I needed to escape former job pressures I was no longer subject to since handing in my resignation the day before.

Instead, I changed plans mid-stream. You couldn't say I was inflexible.

Unable to talk to Allie on a dead phone, Key West would have to wait. I knew it wasn't in any danger of disappearing. I turned west toward

Panama Crossing and Allie. If she needed my help, there was no way I could say no. What she wouldn't—or couldn't—tell me in a text, I hoped she'd be able to tell me in person.

I turned into a rest stop to let Zelda out for her run and found the charge cord. I plugged in and called to let Allie know to expect two for dinner. She sounded disappointed. I didn't take time to let her know my plus-one was a dog.

I also didn't bother checking with Zelda to ask if it was all right if she wouldn't be seeing the sights in Key West.

I figured she'd never know the difference.

Tires rattling on driveway gravel announced our arrival in the marina parking lot. The place was enormous. I got out of the car for a better look. Fresh paint dressed up what was already a good-looking private marina. A flag snapped in the stiff wind, forcing the rope to slap the steel pole. The smell of salt water and the gulf was strong.

Allie met me in the parking lot with a puzzled look and three sweaty Sols to take the edge off. "Where's your passenger?"

"Zelda? She's sleeping in the back."

Allie didn't appear too impressed with my social skills. She gave me a look that said she wanted to bury me in an empty lot. "Will I get to meet her, or are you going to leave her there?"

She returned my shit-eating grin with a scowl, and I knew I better introduce the two of them sooner rather than later. I opened the back door and Zelda sprung up from her doggie dreams and hustled out on all fours. "Zelda, this is Allie. Make nice and maybe she'll let you have some of that beer."

Zelda's cold wet nose sniffled and snuffled its way from Allie's ankles all the way up to her crotch. By the time my favorite girl worked her nose back down to where she started, Zelda's tail was wagging faster than the snapping rope on the flagpole. Both women looked pretty happy.

The dog plopped down on her rear at Allie's feet and looked from me to her and back. Allie reached for Zelda's ear and began scratching and I already knew the best part of my job was done.

All I had left to do was find out what was going on. "Your messages didn't say much. How about filling me in on the dirty details?"

"Let's go in. Chinese is on the way."

Zelda attached herself to Allie, kind of like I had attached myself to the woman back in the old days. I wasn't dumb enough to think there'd be much left between us after I got her arrested for harboring a fugitive. That fugitive was me. She blew town without a word, pretty much guaranteeing that she was pissed at me.

I couldn't blame her.

"I'm sorry about what happened—"

"I know, Jim. It wasn't all your fault. As an employee in the coroner's office, I should have known enough not to get involved."

"And as a cop, I should have known better than to expect you to give me a place to stay, even though you did."

With the apologizing out of the way, it was time to get down to what interrupted the Key West vaycay Zelda and I had planned on. "Until I listened to your messages, I thought you were gone forever."

"So did I, but I'm glad you're here. My brother, Hank, is in the charter boat business. He rents and crews boats to anyone that can afford one. A lot of the business happens in the winter with the snowbirds."

"So this is where you disappeared to. It sounds like nice work if you can get it."

I looked around at the vast compound. I recognized huge boat racks for yachts and the tractors used to move them around. There were racks and racks for smaller boats, too.

"It is, minus the cheats, liars and assorted assholes that don't pay their bills." She rubbed her eyes, as if to block out everything around her.

"I'd say that's pretty standard for someone in business. Does Hank own all this outright?"

"He does. Well, he owns part of it. It's a family business. There's just him and me left." Allie crossed her arms. "But that's not the problem. I'm convinced that at least one, and maybe more, of his captains is running a side business."

In our other lives, Allie and I ended up crossing paths at some of the crime scenes we worked. For whatever reason, we decided we might enjoy spending time together outside of work. She mentioned her brother and how he was all she had after her folks were killed in a car accident. Her brother took over the family business. Allie chose to stay on as one of the city's coroners.

"If the employees are doing something illegal, the entire business could end up forfeited as proceeds of crime. His home, too. Everything."

It became obvious why Allie messaged me. There was a problem with that, though. I knew absolutely nothing about boats. Hell, I couldn't even swim. I figured I'd let her keep talking until she made plain what she wanted.

"I never told my brother about you. I've been on the down-low since getting here. None of the crews know he has a sister."

I got it. Finally. "He's looking for crew, isn't he?"

"Yes. I told him I'd help him out. I didn't tell him anything about you."

"And?"

"I think some of the regulars have been scaring off anyone reliable so they can get more of their own hired on. Hank is desperate for people he can trust. I'm going to sign on as crew. You're going to go down to the dock tomorrow and talk him into signing you."

Over the Chinese food we both liked, Allie briefed me on her brother's operation and filled me in on the details. It wasn't small potatoes. It was high-class. He owned almost a dozen hulls, anywhere from fifty to a hundred feet. A couple of them were cigarettes, capable of high-speed ocean navigation. Or of running people.

And maybe even drugs.

It would be easy to head out into the gulf, meet up with a tramp steamer or a mini-sub and load up with whatever they were carrying. No customs to clear. Nothing but found money.

I didn't let on I knew anything about that.

I hooked up with a dog-friendly motel and checked in with Zelda. In the morning, I put her in a kennel and tried to explain to her it wouldn't be forever. She didn't believe me, so I put out water and a bowl of food to assuage my guilt. It didn't halt the whining. Neither did her fave chew-toy.

That had the exact opposite effect. It pretty much assured her it would be forever.

I made my way to the marina in the quiet, humid early morning air. The flag drooped over the pole. The smell was pleasant. No dead fish odor to spoil the effect.

The office door was open. I walked in and introduced myself to Hank, Allie's brother. He was tall and lanky and tanned from years spent on the gulf with the charter business. I hadn't thought a resumé would be worth much in his line of work. Besides, I was out of my league. For Allie's sake I couldn't turn down her call for help.

Even if I didn't know how to swim.

After a couple of questions and a little back and forth, I convinced Hank I didn't know squat about boats. Maybe he bought my story about wanting a little saltwater adventure in my otherwise dull life. Or maybe he was just desperate enough to give me a chance.

Hank teamed me up with Allie and the two of us went in search of the rest of the crew. We found them gathered at the end of the wharf, in deep conversation. It ended abruptly and silence overtook as we approached. Eyes shifted nervously as we drew closer.

We shared a glance to confirm our suspicions, and then we were on them. Allie introduced me to what looked like some of the toughest, scruffiest-looking old salts on the coast. They might be known for instilling confidence and respect in the outfit's clients, but a couple of the rag-tags looked to be pretty shady. Knives, wristbands and even an eye patch appeared to be the order of the day.

Minus hooks or peg-legs, I wondered how the man with the patch lost the eye.

Two of the men caught my attention right off. Neither Steve nor Dell would look at me straight up. Cop that I was—okay, ex-cop—I took it as a sign. I hadn't been away from the job to have forgotten everything I learned working the streets.

As the newbie, I got my first job. I grabbed the bucket and the brush and began scrubbing down the dock. It didn't take a lot of brain cells to push a scrub brush on a stick. I tackled it with my usual devil-may-care attitude and used the downtime to study the rest of the crew.

It appeared as though Dell and Steve were thick as thieves. Heads bowed, they shared their secrets in barely audible tones. Try as I might, I couldn't make out the back and forth mumbling. I figured it would be those two who would end up being the troublemakers.

If I turned out to be wrong, so be it. There were plenty of other employees to take their place, even if they didn't appear to be capable of doing whatever it was they were doing to the company.

"Where did Allie get to?" My eyes searched the wharf.

"She shipped out with the boys on one of the pontoon boats."

She was getting right to it. That was good. "Did we get a charter?"

"No, I think it's a test run of some sort."

Strange. No one mentioned it earlier.

Rain or shine, as a cop nothing ever changed but whether I'd get wet or sunburned. That's why I never paid attention to the weather, and that's why I never paid attention to the storm blowing in off the Gulf.

If it hit, I'd get wet. If it didn't, I'd stay dry.

I didn't give a thought to what might happen to a pontoon boat. It was a boat. It floated. What could possibly go wrong?

2

The duo striding to my end of the pier sporting wrinkled suit jackets didn't look like they belonged. Their ugly demeanor and dark greasy hair pretty much disqualified them as retired blue-hairs. The bulges under their arms said they were maybe tired cops. Or worse.

No matter. I hadn't been out of the city long enough to ignore them.

"Can I help you?"

"Where's Hank?" one of them asked.

"He's not here yet. Anything I can do?"

Eyes rolled and they looked at me like I was nuts before they shuffled off toward the office. When the door closed, the yelling started. I dropped back into deckhand mode and went back to worrying if Allie would make it back before the storm blew in.

I wanted to move into a position that would allow me to eavesdrop, but Steve and Dell were back to mumbling. I sidestepped closer, trying to catch the gist of their conversation. Rather than wait for me to get there, they approached me.

"We've got a proposal for you."

Oh-oh. Here we go. "Then let's talk."

They led me to the end of the wharf. On the way I wondered what the two of them would come up with. By the time I got there, the look of the sky and the howling wind diverted my thoughts once again to Allie and the pontoon boat she shipped out on.

I didn't know squat about water, but the gulf was a gigantic body of it. It was big enough to make its own weather, and that was what it looked like it was doing. For now, the onshore sky was clear and blue. In the direction Allie headed off to, the ceiling was low and almost black, and the clouds were bound for shore.

I listened to Steve and Dell spin their tale of woe. When they finished, I had all the information I needed to begin a proper investigation. Hell, they did such a good job of it, I hardly had any questions—except for one. "Who are you working for?"

"We can't tell you that. We know who Allie is, though. And we think you're the ex-cop she used to go out with back east."

"Okay then. You're DEA or Immigration or both. Maybe with ATF thrown in for good measure, although I already know one can't represent the other."

"You might be right, but you're not going to find out from us."

"If you're local, you probably knew about or grew up with Hank. That means you know him personally. Is he the kind of guy to get mixed up in whatever it is brought you two here?"

"We don't think so. We think someone is holding something over him."

"I agree. That's pretty much the way Allie told it, too." By now I was damned sure they knew more than they were letting on. My impatience was growing. Concern about Allie out in the pontoon boat in the growing storm didn't help matters. "So now what, gentlemen?"

Black cloud dropped low and got even darker, if that was possible. The accompanying wind unleashed a driving rain. Hulls strained against moorings and rocked back and forth, banging hard against fenders. Ignorant as I was about ocean storms, this one looked like it would get pretty intense, even to me.

I worried about Allie in the pontoon boat. Like I needed another woman in my life disappearing, whether or not it was my fault. With the wind picking up, I was concerned for her safety on the water in a floating cork of a boat that would make a pretty good sail.

"When this storm blows over, we're going looking for the pontoon boat. If it's out in the middle of this blow, there's no telling where it could end up."

Steve corrected me. "They're called squalls."

In a matter of minutes, the wind turned to vicious. I put my back to it and worked my way off the dock onto shore, rocking and rolling all the way. Once inside the shelter of the boathouse, hail and anything that wasn't tied down slapped against the tin roof and sides. Almost as quick as it blew in, the squall moved inland and dissipated, and Steve gave his orders.

"I'll go tell Hank where we're going. Jim, you and Dell get the engine warmed up."

Shit. Now Dell would find out for sure I knew squat about boats.

"How much experience do you have?" Dell asked.

I couldn't fault him for asking. Better to admit it than to be thought the fool. "None."

"We figured. Okay, first things first. Where's the wind?"

That was an easy one. "It's blowing the boat against the pier."

"Yes it is. If it was blowing the other way, it would be a lot simpler. The wind would end up blowing the boat clear of the dock."

"So what do we do?"

"First, you'll cast off all the lines but the one attaching the bow. When you've done that, watch and listen to what Steve does with the after bow spring line. He'll show you where to stow everything after we get under way."

"I have no idea what you're talking about."

"You'll learn or drown."

"I hope not."

"Once we're underway, you can pull the fenders in."

My job was to watch and learn, so that's what I did. With the bow attached by means of the after bow spring, Dell used the rudder and the engine to swing the stern away from the dock. Steve cast off the spring line, and we reversed away from the dock.

Piece of cake when someone knew what they were doing.

The squall had blown itself out, but I was still anxious about Allie. Maybe I should have felt the same way about the rest of them on the pontoon, too. I didn't, particularly after Steve filled me in on the experience level of the boat's crew. Old salts, all of them.

"How are we going to find them?" I asked.

"There's only a handful of places they could put in. Dell is going to stand watch with the binoculars," Steve confirmed.

I had to ask again. "Do you still think Allie is a part of whatever Hank is involved in?

"No. She has nothing to do with any of it. Her brother might be another matter."

That was a relief, although I wouldn't have expected anything else. I knew her to be a straight arrow. I also knew she wasn't so sure about her brother.

We readied the fastboat for a rescue run and I contributed what I could by bringing in fenders. Steve piloted while Dell scoured the shoreline with the glasses, searching for the pontoon. A couple of false alarms and his arm moved up and down once more. Steve aimed the boat toward shore for the third time.

Whoever beached left the stern sticking far out into the river. The engine was left to idle. Our boat couldn't get in close. I jumped ship and waded through the shallows. I scrambled aboard. Muffled cries greeted me. Allie lay sprawled on the deck, hands and ankles bound.

I undid the gag and she couldn't stop talking.

"Those sons of bitches. If I ever get my hands on them—"

"Slow down. Are they still here?" I wanted to know.

"No. They met another boat. They left me tied up and pointed it toward shore. Whatever they had in bags—drugs or cash or both—disappeared with them."

So it was drugs, after all. I figured it to be as much in this part of the world. Out of the way, yet not entirely isolated, it was a perfect place for pretending to enjoy a little boating pastime while doing some smuggling.

"They know about you, Jim. They know you're a cop. One of them recognized you as the cop who sent him up."

So much for the anonymity I hoped for. "Too bad I can't remember them all or I'd have seen it coming. I'll check names on Hank's roster. If I have any friends on the local PD it shouldn't take long to get answers."

Allie paced back and forth, still angry with herself for getting fooled. "I should have known, dammit. I should have known."

"Stop beating yourself up. There's no way you could have."

She held that thought and it seemed to slow her down. "I think there might be some Sol left in the cooler if the bastards didn't steal that, too. It's going to be a long haul to get this slow boat back to port."

She had me with the Sol. While we were talking, Dell and Steve managed to work their boat to shore. They didn't say no either, even if company rules said they shouldn't. Before we popped the tops we affixed a towline to the pontoon boat and tugged it free.

"Come on, landlubber," Allie said. "You're riding with me on the pontoon. We have some talking to do if you're going to be working here."

I looked at Dell and Steve. Their heads shook in unison with hang-dog looks. I knew from experience there was more going on than I could fathom.

My new-found career as a wharf rat was turning out to vastly differ from the one I knew as a police detective.

Allie eased the pontoon against the dock exactly at midnight. We tied up under a curtain of bright, star-filled sky. Thanks to the sunshine, fresh air and the warm tropical breeze that replaced the chilly rain that fell earlier in the day, I could barely keep my eyes open.

The belly full of Sol didn't help. All I wanted to do was head back to the no-tell motel and crash.

"You might as well collect your gear and move into my place," Allie offered. "The cat is out of the bag by the look of it."

"Are you sure? My record with women hasn't been all that great since you left town."

"I heard, and from what I remember, it wasn't all that great before I left, either, landlubber."

I couldn't deny it. "You got me there."

"What did you do with Zelda?"

"I put her in a kennel for safekeeping since I didn't know what I was walking into."

Allie's hands moved to her hips. She tapped a foot for emphasis. "Do you treat all your women like that?

"Only the ones I love."

"We'll just have to see about that."

We sat in silence at the very end of the pier, away from the lights. Exhausted, we dangled our feet in the water. It might not be magic, but it was a wonderful substitute after the day we spent retrieving the beached pontoon.

Allie had only just rested her head on my shoulder when the sound of gunfire brought us to our senses. I caught a muzzle flash out of the corner of my eye and zeroed in on something I hoped wasn't meant for us. The water around us began to splash and I knew that not to be the case.

"Shit. It's tough wearing an ankle piece in shorts. My regular is tucked away in the car." I grabbed Allie's hand and pulled her off the wharf toward shore and cover. I shoved her behind a stack of pallets. "Stay here and keep down."

The muzzle flashes were coming from farther down the swampy shoreline. In the inky blackness it was difficult to tell exactly where. We must have made for easy targets beneath the dock lights. I thought maybe the shooter was only trying to scare us.

If that was the case, it worked.

I sprinted toward the dark parking lot and popped the trunk. I grabbed my automatic and the two large-capacity mags and slammed the trunk closed. I steered the car through the obstacle course to get to Allie. I tried swapping out the shorty magazine while I was driving, but that didn't make the dodging any easier.

I reached Allie, jammed the gearshift into park and waited while she dove into the back seat. Another bright muzzle-flash let me locate the source of the gunfire. I dialed in full auto, stuck the muzzle out the window, and unleashed the thirty-three-round mag in its general direction.

As it always had in the past, silence ensued. Mission accomplished, even though I knew I wasn't close to hitting anything that mattered. "Let's see if we can pick up Zelda. Then we can head over to your place."

"We're already at my place," she insisted.

"No, I mean where you live, woman."

"This is it, buster."

"In that case, Zelda will have to wait until tomorrow. What's company policy on pets?"

"You'll have to deal with the owner on that one, but I'd say it's looking to be pretty lenient. As long as Zelda is the only other woman in your life, that is."

"She's the only one left alive from my recent past," I assured her.

Even in the dark I could sense Allie's hesitation in making a decision she might later regret. Then she said it. "For now, that will have to do."

It felt good to wash away my sins in the shower after spending the better part of the day in salt air. Good woman that she was, by the time everything went down the drain, Allie had sandwiches waiting.

I tried not to talk with my mouth full. I wasn't successful.

"So far, you've got two ex-employees who made a delivery of cash or drugs on one of your boats. With you on board. Any idea why you had to be there?"

"I don't think they were expecting me. I jumped on the pontoon at the last minute."

"Are you sure your brother isn't involved in any of this? Is the business solvent?" The question had to be asked.

"Yes, as far as I know. But now that you asked, I'll do some basic accounting. I'll be back in a bit. You'll have to find the bedroom on your own for now."

The for now sounded promising.

My pleasure at the thought ended abruptly when the dream I was having ended. Allie was sitting on the edge of the bed and she didn't look happy. Perhaps it was her puzzled look. I sat up. "So, what's the deal?"

"I took a quick look. It appears as though Hank owes money."

"How much?"

"He's making good cash on the boat charters. He's even making it on the dive charters."

"How much?"

"I couldn't tell for sure. It looks like it started about three weeks before I got here."

"How much?"

"You're just like a dog with a bone. It must be the ex-cop in you. About fifty thousand."

At last. "That's not so bad. If he's making money, he should be able to change his payments with the bank.

"You're right, he should be able to. One problem, though."

"Don't tell me. He doesn't owe any banks," I surmised.

"Pretty much."

"If the money he's making is good, why would he borrow the cash from people like that?"

"I have no idea, Jim, but first thing tomorrow, I'll be asking."

Sleep didn't come easy, even under the air conditioning. Even with Allie's cool body beside mine. I kept trying to put it all together long after her even breathing told me she was fast asleep.

So far, there were two people who said they were feds, both on the company payroll. Maybe they weren't feds. Maybe they were there to monitor Hank's payback program. I wanted to ask Allie if she knew anything about Steve and Dell.

Instead, I let her sleep.

Two former employees buggered off with a boat and a shitload of cash or drugs or both. I wanted to know more. I eased out of bed, dressed, and headed down to the pontoon boat for a closer look.

The batteries in the flashlight were dead by the time I finished the cursory search. That wasn't a major problem, though. The sun rising over the horizon gave me more light than I needed to make a more thorough job of it.

3

The smell of Allie's fresh coffee drifting through the trailer roused me out of bed. While I dressed, I hoped for something more substantial. I finished dressing and made my way to the kitchen. I opened the fridge door. Pickings appeared to be slim to none.

Allie had a plan, though. She always did.

"There's a little café down the road. I'll treat you to breakfast for your troubles."

"Zelda and I are on the lookout for a cook. After the impromptu feast you did up last night, I figured man and dog were home-free. Now you tell us you're not cooking."

"I need to get away from this place after what happened yesterday. We'll pick up Zelda and groceries on the way back."

We ended up in a booth at an old-style diner covered with stainless steel on the outside and the

1950s on the inside. Like most diners, the staple was mostly good food and a waitress with an affinity for local gossip. The older woman who appeared to have worked there forever dished out food with abandon to what looked like the regulars.

We killed time with small talk until the food arrived and we could converse without interruption.

"Tell me what you know about Dell and Steve," I said.

"Not much. Hank says they've been around for a while. They know the business. They have a nautical background and they're certified divers."

That's all she got out before the explosion boomed and thundered, echoing inside the diner's tin walls. I grabbed Allie's hand and pulled her out the door and down the steps. The cloud of black smoke blossomed skyward from where we had been only minutes before.

"That doesn't look good. Come on."

We ran all the way to arrive at the boathouse. The fire department was already turning into the marina and a passing fire boat was floating off the dock. Damage appeared to be limited to a locked storage area out of sight behind the main building. The bomb squad arrived shortly after. So did Steve.

"Is the bomb squad your doing?"

"It is. I thought they might find something I couldn't."

"I tore through the pontoon boat last night." I pulled out the map I found and unfolded it.

Steve took a look and tapped his finger on several of the marks that were circled.

"I know some of these places. They're out of the way. Most wouldn't bother with them."

"Which makes them good for conducting business of one sort or another," I said.

"I'd say so."

"Given what you've learned so far, would it be drugs or illegals?"

Steve didn't hesitate. "Could be both."

Steve's cover-your-ass logic didn't impress me. Given how long both he and his partner Dell had been here, that was the best they could come up with? I could be wrong, but it was looking like they were on a club fed paid vaycay.

It was that, or they were deliberately holding out.

"How do you propose we find out?" I asked.

The pissed-off look crossing Allie's face said she'd had enough. I couldn't blame her. The actions of her brother could end up costing her the family business on account of his drug dealings.

"You guys figure it out for yourselves. I'm going to pick up Zelda."

Like Steve and Dell, I was no help either. In fact, so far, the only constructive thing I'd done was cut some duct tape off of Allie.

The last words I heard were, Who's Zelda?

At one point, Hank, Allie's brother, held all the marbles in the business. Now he owed 50K on it, and by the look and sound of the explosion, his payments had to be running late. If the bombing wasn't a warning from those Hank owed money, it would be a feeble way to take down a building.

I put a hold on the human trafficking horse-manure and went with the drug scenario. The fifty might not be big enough to kill anyone over, at least not a business owner that had assets such as expensive boats that could be put to use. It would be enough to send a message by blowing up an outbuilding. And speaking of that, where the hell was Hank?

With Allie out of the way temporarily while she went to retrieve Zelda, it was time to put the pressure on Steve to pony up. I found him on the dock. "You need to level with me."

He wasn't happy to see me. "Look, I know you have skin in the game, but I don't have much to tell. Even if you are an ex-cop. Yeah, I know, I checked you out."

So he knew. I wondered how much he already told the rest of Hank's crew. "Then you must have found out I don't take kindly to fools. By the look of it, both you and Dell have been putting in quite a bit of time on this little project."

"You don't know shit," Steve said.

"I know your tan lines are dark, your hair is long, and the sunglasses make you both look like a couple of surfers from California that took a wrong turn. I'd say that line works pretty good on the weekend crowd of Miami girls."

"It takes time to work up an investigation of this magnitude," he insisted.

"Maybe, but I'm here and learning fast. You start your weekends early on Friday to make the long road trip into Miami. You don't get back until Monday. How am I doing so far?" I had him, and he knew it.

"Well—"

I'd made it plain I knew their game. "Well, nothing. It's looking like it's one long vaycay for both of you. That makes for only a three-day work week to break up the monotony and collect the paycheck."

I laid on the finishing touch. "I've got some connections in places you probably know. I think I'll make a few phone calls to see what I can find out about what's going on."

"All right, you win. Dial it back a notch, all right?"

Steve as much as admitted they'd been screwing the pooch. Once Zelda got here, she'd have a hard time keeping both of them off of her. I hoped Zelda wouldn't be catching their fleas. Or anyone else, as far as that goes.

"Are you saying you're not after Hank? Having his assets forfeited would be quite a catch on someone's record." I thought it was a pretty good guess.

"It's not Hank we're after. He's a small-time user who got lucky with too much credit. His supplier must have seen the scope of Hank's business and thought he might be able to pick it up on the cheap. It's the higher-ups that really interest us. We want to know where Hank's supplier is getting it."

I flipped the recorder out of my pocket and made a show of letting the man see it. His ashen face about said everything. "I'll be holding you to that."

I figured Allie wouldn't be in the best frame of mind by the time I climbed the stairs to her apartment. Still, she retrieved Zelda and fed her. Both of them were curled up in a tight fit on the sofa. Zelda was having her ears scratched. It was a toss-up who had the biggest grin.

Okay, so maybe Allie's mood wasn't the worst. My smile was pretty big, too. I knew I'd have to dive right in while things were looking good. "Your brother—"

Allie nodded in the direction of the kitchen and sat up. Zelda knew enough to scurry off the sofa. She plopped down to face us and looked from me to Allie and back like she knew something we didn't.

"I know all about it. Hank. Get in here."

Poor Hank shuffled into the room, head hanging and by the look of it, knees shaking. I was too glad that Allie's anger wasn't directed toward me, or I'd be in the same boat with the knees.

"Hank, this is Jim Nash. He's here to help me. And by extension, you. Do you get it?"

Hank looked to be a walking disaster. The sweaty, pale face was only surpassed by the sweat that soaked through his shirt. His hands shook and his face twitched. It wasn't just that his sister was ragging on him. He looked to be coming down off a binge that must have lasted the past two days.

"You're a weekend binger, aren't you?" It wasn't really a question. He looked at me like I was from another planet. He looked like he didn't want to answer, either.

"Pretty much."

At last. "Ever inject?"

"No".

"How long have you been using?"

"About six months, off and on," he admitted.

"That 50K you owe, is that for yourself, or for parties?"

Allie's brother deflated and shrunk about a foot. His eyes looked anywhere but at me. I was pretty sure he wanted to crawl into a corner and die. Instead, he turned away from his sister and faced me. "Parties, mostly. I could never use that by myself."

"Some could. You know the next line of that shit could kill you, right? Or the one after that, or the one after that."

"I never thought of it that way," he admitted.

"Start."

It was plain to me Hank was hurting. It wouldn't be long before he'd be crashing, and crashing hard. Suspicion and paranoia wouldn't be far behind. What also wouldn't be far behind was the desire for more coke to stuff up his nose to ease the symptoms, funded by ever more of the business.

Allie heard enough. "Hank, you need to get out of here and into rehab."

"I won't go into rehab," he told her. "We can't afford it. I can do it on my own."

"No, you can't. The problem is this: You owe money. They know where you live. They already sent you a message with the shed blowing up."

He started to pay attention. Eyes and ears pointed in my direction. Even Zelda looked up at me. "What? What happened?"

The man didn't know. I filled him in. "Yesterday someone sent you a message by blowing up a storage area."

Hank came back to earth. It was painful to watch. It was obvious he realized it could have been worse. "Shit. I know I can do this if Allie is here to help me. I'm only a weekend user."

I heard that often enough. Mind you, I didn't know him. I didn't know what he was capable of. Plus, there was the whole bomb thing. It went from bad to worse.

Hank turned to his sister. "Allie. Say something."

I knew when Hank said it. It was the wrong thing to say. Allie looked at me, and then at her brother and back at me. She got up off the sofa, pulled back her right and hit Hank with a pile-driver that I thought would knock him sober. In fact, it just might have. When the shock worked its way through, Hank climbed up off the floor and hugged his sister. The tears were my cue.

"Come on, Zelda. It's time to go for a walk." My dog didn't waste time making for the door. Neither did I.

The light offshore breeze eased the humidity out to sea and replaced it with cooler and drier air. It was bearable to be outside. Even Zelda appreciated it. I could tell by the way she wagged her tail.

Well, all right. I couldn't tell. It just seemed like it.

The truck nonchalantly pulled out from the curb. Until the headlights pointed directly at us, I wasn't sure. Zelda didn't have any doubt. If it depended on me, we'd have been road kill.

The truck missed by the hair of my chinny-chin-chin and roared past. I was so happy to be here that it never occurred to me to get the plate. When I came to my senses, it was too late.

"Come on, Zelda, I think we better double-time it home to momma before someone gets lucky."

I spoke too soon.

The second vehicle came out from a cross-street and bore down on us from behind. This time, the racing engine clued me in. I yanked Zelda behind a pole and together we watched the sideshow as the driver stuck his head out the window. Maybe he thought he was a dog out for a drive to bask in some fresh air.

He cranked fast on the wheel to keep the car headed in our direction. The engine revved. Tires squealed and lost traction. The car swerved, bumped against the curb, and flipped onto its roof.

This was getting too easy. The dust cleared and I tried forcing the door. It caught, scraped against the pavement and jammed. I gave up and reached in through the open window. I had to fish through two pockets before I came up with ID.

The third pocket wasn't empty, either. My hand filled with an automatic. I checked the action and tucked the handgun into my belt.

"All right, Zelda, let's carry on with our walk. I don't think anyone will bother us for the rest of it. And if they do—"

I patted the handgun.

Zelda must have agreed, because she wagged her tail and nosed my hand. Either that, or she was looking for a treat for her well-done job of saving my ass yet again.

It occurred to me that Hank had his head in just a little deeper than he was willing to admit. Launching two cars at someone was definitely overkill, especially if the first would have done its job. Either the bums were extremely incompetent, or it was a double warning.

For now, I'd be going with incompetent.

I couldn't figure where the two feds fit into the scheme of things. I didn't know where Dell and Steve were coming from. It seemed like they were out for themselves with a shortened schedule and weekend trips to Miami. I wondered if they'd be around when the chips were down, and if they were, how much good it would do.

So far, I had a kidnapping, a shooting, an explosion, and two cars attempting to run me over. None of it got me any closer to figuring out what the hell was going on.

First out of bed in my house meant cooking breakfast. Last out of bed had better make it. Fortunately for all of us, Zelda couldn't cook, but I could. Allie would have to be happy with bed duty.

Yeah. No. I left out the part that said it wasn't my house. I figured if I knew what was good for me, I'd act like I did. I didn't get to turn on the stove. Allie came out of the bedroom dressed for work. When I checked, the bed wasn't made either. I'd have to work on that, given the chance.

"What's up?" I wanted to know.

"I just got a phone call. Someone wants to reserve a boat to take an offshore trip to meet up with a freighter."

"Is that normal?" I wanted to know.

"Not really."

"It doesn't sound right, Allie."

"I know. But business is business. We need the money, Nash."

"Which boat?"

"The cigarette."

The cigarette was a sleek, fast boat. A go-fast. Images of the old Miami Vice television show came to mind.

"Will you fuel and warm it up for me?"

I headed downstairs in the pier's direction and the expensive cigarette moored at the end. Whoever hired it wanted speed. I filled the tank, checked the oil and started the fans. After a few minutes of warm-up, she'd be good to go in a hurry.

The dock gate slammed and Dell joined me. The gun in his hand wasn't reassuring. He waved it in the direction of shore and I led the way up the stairs. At his car he popped the trunk and smacked me on the back of the head.

He pushed me forward and I dropped into it like a side of beef.

4

At first, I wasn't sure if it was my head buzzing or the sound of the cigarette at full throttle leaving the dock in its wake. I didn't care, though, because the first thing I needed to do was find the trunk's release handle in the dark.

I ignored my pounding head and flailed and kicked and felt around until I connected with it in the dark confines of the trunk. I yanked and the lid popped open. Modern cars. You can't beat them.

Blinded by the light, I blinked and squinted until my eyesight went back to normal. I threw a leg over the back of the car and found solid ground.

Dizzy and disorientated from the gun-barrel to the head, I stumbled and fell back. I barely kept from falling. Whatever I was trying to do, it didn't work. I couldn't hold myself steady. On my way down, I made a grab for the dirt and planted my face firmly.

Steady as she goes, even if I was spread-eagled on the ground.

I pulled myself to my feet and stumbled in the general direction of my car. I fished for the keys and opened the trunk and managed not to dive in and face-plant. I fumbled for my automatic and the magazines. The familiar firepower saved my ass too many times to count. The mere sound of it unloading was cause enough to force a shooter to turn tail and hide.

The second cigarette boat was still moored. It would be my only chance of catching up with Allie. I stumbled down the wooden dock and only went down on my knees once. I didn't even pick up a sliver for my troubles.

I checked the fuel and started the fans to clear the engine compartment. Impatient as I was, the last thing I wanted was to blow the boat sky-high with me in it.

The prevailing wind held me hard against the dock. I didn't have time to practice what I'd already been taught. Instead, I reversed and spun the wheel enough times to get pointed in the direction I needed to be going. As soon as I got clear of the dock, I firewalled the twin throttles on the sleek, powerful cigarette.

I cleared the breakwater at full speed, but the only thing on the horizon that I could see appeared ghostly, obscured by the salt-water haze whipped up from the foamy, wind-driven waves. I checked my aim and locked the wheel.

For a guy who didn't know shit from Shinola about boating, I thought things were going swimmingly right up until the strong, on-shore wind forced the bow hard against the pounding waves. My head throbbed in unison, still aching from the rap on the back of the head.

The boat topped an enormous wave and I caught sight of what I was chasing. Already Allie's cigarette was on its return run toward shore. I unlocked the wheel and cranked it hard. I thought for sure I'd be able to come around in a matching arc. What I hadn't thought about was what I'd do when I caught up.

It was all going pretty well until it wasn't.

The landlubber part of me had no understanding that being broadside to wind and wave at speed might create some questionable rock-and-roll where it wasn't wanted. I grabbed on to everything I could. Being too stupid to panic probably saved me from going into the drink.

The bobbing cork I found myself on didn't settle down until I had her pointed downwind. She resumed a more regular up-and-down crashing through and then overtop of wave after wave. My ignorance saved me yet again.

Each time the boats descended into the swells separating them, I lost sight of everything. Without a constant reference, I grew confused, angry, and lost every time. To add insult to injury, both engines stumbled and quit, leaving me at the mercy of the fierce wind driving the angry sea.

Adrift, the boiling sea and waves rolling higher and faster than an amusement park thrill-ride had me clinging to the boat like it was the last I'd ever see of solid ground. Except it wasn't solid, and it wasn't ground. Water poured in and sloshed, ankle-deep and rising. Wind driving the saltwater spray blanked my vision.

Blinded, on my knees, trying to hang on and not get thrown overboard by the constant shifting and uneven rocking of the boat became my primary goal. Rather than let panic take over, I ran through a check-list of my own making.

It was a short one. I needed to get an engine going. Still reeling, I lurched forward and punched a starter. When nothing happened, I took a break and wrapped rope around my waist and tied off. If I was going to go down, it would be with the boat.

I tried the second engine.

Still nothing. I fumbled with the throttles and jammed one into neutral. I tried again and an engine caught and fired. I rammed the single throttle forward.

Secure in the knowledge that for now I wouldn't be drowning within sight of land, I completely forgot about the second engine. The heavy boat lurched its way toward shore, underpowered and forced to plow through wave after wave.

The only thing I knew about boats, I learned watching movies and television. Something screamed bilge pump. I frantically searched the dash for a switch that I knew should be somewhere. I found two, and punched them up.

That reminded me I might have a second engine to try and get started.

I adjusted the throttle and repeated the start sequence for number two. It caught right away. With both engines and the bilge pumps doing their duty, the level of the water washing into the boat began slowly subsiding. Not long after it was back to ankle-deep.

For only a moment I was convinced that a sliver of sunlight escaped through the cloud and shone down on me. Either that, or I was delirious.

By now, I had no idea where I was. I couldn't make out the shoreline. The boat I was in a hurry to catch disappeared along with it.

I continued pointing the bow downwind and hoped for the best.

On the verge of surrendering and heading back to where I thought the marina should be, I topped a wave. Through the haze, a boat popped up in front of me. It looked to be stopped, but with the wind and the waves and the rocking and rolling roller-coaster ride I was taking, I couldn't be sure. I had a suspicion that whatever I was looking at, it couldn't be good.

At first, I didn't recognize the two shapeless blobs squatting in the middle of the ocean. I drew closer and thought I could make out a tiny sand-spit barely above water. It took a couple of minutes of speeding toward it to finally recognize those blobs for what they were.

Sharks, perhaps. Or porpoises. Or I don't know what. In the blinding, wind-driven salt spray and thick haze, it didn't occur to me they could be people. As far as I knew, people couldn't walk on water.

Not even Allie.

Howling wind drove the waves crashing over the sand-spit into a hellish, foaming maelstrom. Hope of beaching to retrieve what I finally recognized as two people seemed impossible. They were trying to hold onto a spit of sand by digging into it for dear life.

I had no time to stay scared of what I knew would be inevitable. I had no idea what would be necessary. I didn't know how to handle a boat, not in screaming wind and crashing waves and rough sea. In that instant I knew we were all going to drown.

I steered past the spit and came around into wind to slowly move up parallel to the sand-spit. I tossed out useless life jackets that got lost in the wind. I reduced power and allowed the boat to be blown back by the wind.

Cursing, I couldn't understand why no one attempted to make a grab for the life jackets. It only made sense when I recognized that both were trying to hang on to nothing more than sand. It was that, or they would be washed away into the sea.

At least whoever forced them to walk the plank had been gracious enough not to tie them up. If they had, by now they'd be long past drowning in the maelstrom of water and foam crashing over the spit. Or washed away, never to be seen again.

Allie and Steve must have been in shock at seeing another boat stumbling along at just the right time. Unfortunately for them, it was piloted by someone who had no idea how to get them aboard and out of danger. If I was lucky, I'd get one try at rescue.

I tossed out the feeble anchor on the windward side of the spit. The landlubber in me had to figure a way to work the boat over to the downwind side and stay attached. If I could come up on the spit using the engines, maybe they could use the anchor rope to climb on board.

I took the chance.

Waves crashed over the bow, forcing water into every orifice. Salt stung my eyes and forced them into slits. I tried wiping with a hand, but it only made the salt sting worse.

I fought with the throttles. I struggled to keep the bow pointed into the wind. I reduced power.

The wind pushed me backwards. I prayed the anchor rope would be long enough.

It had to be. I had nothing else.

I allowed the boat to drift downwind and experimented with the throttles to find an equilibrium against the wind and the sea crashing over the bow. Each time I worked my way close, wind gusts took over and I was forced to ease back and start over.

My incompetence coupled with the fear that I'd be letting two people drown forced me to keep trying. Again and again I had to abandon my setup to the wind and the waves. Suddenly and without warning, the wind abruptly changed direction. The boat slammed onto the spit and tipped onto its side.

Allie and Steve were exhausted by their efforts to cling to the disappearing sand-spit. Steve used the last of his strength to push Allie over the rail. I made a grab for her and almost fell overboard but for the rope around my waist securing me to the boat. I regained my balance and helped pull Steve on board.

Steve handed over a knife and I sawed through the anchor rope. Just as suddenly, the boat righted itself and re-floated as the sea continued to crash over the sand-spit.

My job now was to get us all back to shore. I firewalled the throttles and set course in a wide arc that would move us safely downwind and home.

I checked the lights above the bilge switches. If we got lucky, the pumps would keep doing their job until we made the breakwater.

Allie's finger dug into my ribs. She motioned me to move aside. I was more than eager. I deserted the admiral of the fleet position in a hurry and allowed her to take over.

She took us inside the breakwater where the wind died and the sea calmed. Only minutes before we had been hostage to deadly forces over open water. The low, black cloud base remaining overhead was the only thing that remained to remind us.

Well, there was that, and my shaking knees.

Steve was first to recover his voice, and his strength. "You're a sight for sore eyes-and I mean that literally. I can't wipe the salt out of them."

I spoke thorough chattering teeth. "If I knew what I was doing, I wouldn't have been out there in the first place."

Allie remained at the controls, steadying herself with the back of her legs jammed against the seat. "You just made Captain, Jim. Unfortunately, thanks to recent budget cuts, there's no pay to go along with it."

I held up shaking hands. "I'm just happy to be here."

I got a lot happier when I thought I caught sight of the boat I'd been chasing moored at a dock. "That looks like the cigarette boat that forced you to walk the plank."

I gestured at what looked like a deserted warehouse jutting out over the water. The clean lines of the cigarette stuck out like a lighthouse beacon on a dark night.

Allie eased the throttles back to just above idle and allowed the boat to drift with the current past the dilapidated building.

"Slow this thing down. I have business to take care of." I grabbed my automatic and two magazines and eased my way across the bow. "Set me on that green patch and this landlubber will forgive you for testing my abilities. I'll see both of you back at the dock."

Steve gave me an Aye, Captain, and I was happy to jump ship onto a narrow patch of solid ground. It wasn't so long ago I thought I'd never be seeing that again. I waded through thick salt grass and spongy, wet shoreline, lifting my feet and planting them carefully.

The building wasn't much to look at. Single-story. About a hundred long by fifty wide. Big enough to hold whatever was going on. No doubt it was chosen for its isolation and beat-up, broken-down unused look.

Blaring music filtering out from inside killed my chances of listening in on any conversation. Bright light shone through a window. Whatever it was, it needed a lot of light.

I bellied my way toward the only window I could see. I figured I'd be up to my ass in alligators in a matter of seconds.

I got a look inside. It was enough to tell me this one-man assault was going to need more planning. I crouched down and crawled my way around all three landward sides of the building. The only way in and out was through the original entrance overlooking the water. The rear was closed up tight. Opposing windows on two sides gave clear views into the building.

I took another quick glance inside and I knew this place was more than I could handle. I crawled off into the bush on my belly and hoped I wouldn't get an opportunity to wrestle with a gator on the lookout for a fresh, warm meal.

I reached into a pocket and pulled out my waterlogged phone. I chanced it and called Allie's phone. Miraculously, the call went through and I asked her to hand the phone off to Steve.

There wasn't much to explain. The cigarette was still moored. I didn't know what I was looking at through the window. A bunch of machinery, and people. It definitely wasn't a meth lab.

I listened to Steve's advice and didn't argue. I took it.

I swatted at mosquitoes. Daydreamed about the vacation in Key West I didn't get to share with Zelda. Tried not to doze off. No way did I want to become fresh food for the alligators I knew had to be loitering. Every sound had me on edge and wondering if they could smell. I told myself they couldn't.

I wasn't stupid enough to believe it.

It seemed like about a day later before a swat team in three boats finally idled its way toward the building. I stayed concealed by the tall grass. The men scrambled off the boats and ran down the dock toward the broken-down building. They surrounded it with practiced ease.

On signal, flash-bangs and tear gas cartridges shattered windows and exploded inside the building. I counted at least a dozen people double-timing their way out, arms held high hoping lead wouldn't fly in their direction.

When I figured the operation was over, I stashed my illegal mags under a mango and strolled onto the dock. Following a pat-down, Steve was more than happy to let me in on the secrets discovered during the search.

He led me on a walk-through. I couldn't count the lathes and boxes of parts for the made-to-order weaponry. Illegal arms were being received, modified to order, and shipped throughout Central America and Mexico. Drug cartels paid good money for that stuff.

It was going to be a feather in Steve's cap to be a party to the discovery. I figured it couldn't hurt to be the one who brought him in on it.

Allie's grin pretty much said it all by the time I arrived back at the wharf. I was unscathed but for the seawater I'd soaked up and the alligators I thought I'd heard wanting to eat me. She almost put us both in the drink in her enthusiasm to welcome me. As for Zelda, well, there was no holding her back, either.

Allie had good news about her brother, too.

"Hank has agreed to go into rehab. He's leaving tomorrow."

"That's a good thing. I'm glad to hear it."

"Just to be sure, he booked two sessions. Back-to-back."

"Smart man. So then, that means you're in charge, does it?"

"Yes, I am. Want to make something of it?" Allie asked.

"No. I was wondering, though—"

"Then wonder no more. I need a dependable man to run herd on the crowd of misfits I suddenly find myself responsible for."

"I know absolutely nothing about boats or dive shops. Or tiki bars, for that matter."

"That makes you perfect for the job, James. I can train you."

"In that case, I have a few ideas—" I began.

"Stow it, landlubber. There'll be plenty of time for that down the road."

"That's what I'm afraid of."

Zelda chose exactly that moment to bark. If she agreed, how could I say no?

Check out all six books of the Harry Delaney Adventure series. Learn why Harry makes his way from the North African desert to the Mexican Baja. Discover how he ends up having a triumphal return to the deserts of North Africa.

About the author

Peter Duke is a Canadian author. He resides and writes in Canada in a small college town in Southern Ontario.

Peter's gypsy spirit has taken him to some strange places in the world, but now he's content to limit his adventures to riding a motorcycle and whatever he might encounter when he's on the road. Consequently, he's worked in bike shops doing odd jobs from planning and putting on rides down Mexico way, taking care of computer networking and security, and to picking up and delivering motorcycles from the L.A. basin to Las Vegas, among other things.

He's ridden over a lot of North America at one time or another from Canada to Mexico, and from Atlantic to Pacific. By far his favorite ride is up and down the length of the Baja Peninsula, where the people are friendly, the sun always shines and it's warm in the winter.

Of everything that he has experienced in his all-too-brief life, Africa is perhaps the greatest enigma. It's a beautiful continent, rich in people, nature and resources, yet poor in all of those areas, too.

pxduke.com

peterxduke@gmail.com

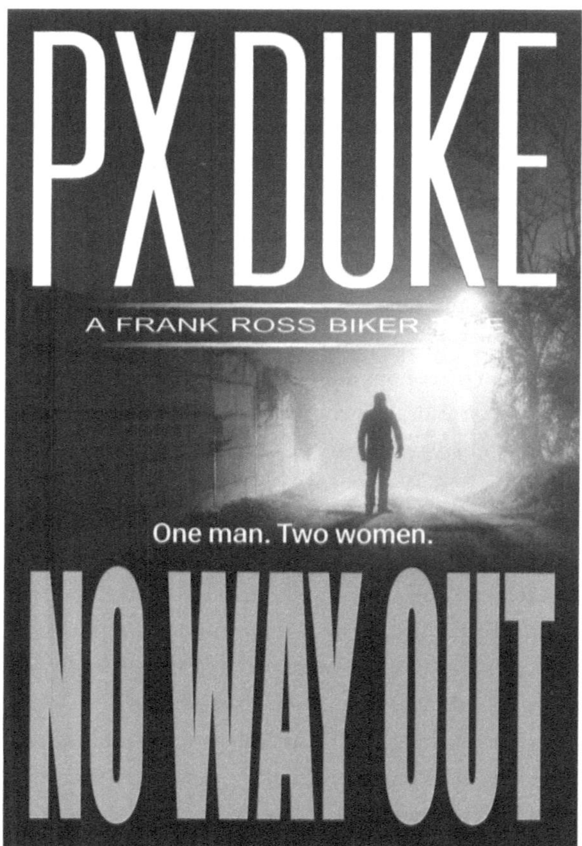

Frank Ross is out of Mexico riding north. He's just across la línea looking for shade and water. He finds it, and a lot more than he bargained for when he breaks down at a casino by the Salton Sea.